Praise for *Lands*

'This book is truly a remarkable
of unhurried, exquisitely paced
universal themes such as love, ...p
with particularly Australian themes such as colonial violence,
inter-racial relationships, Indigenous history, and reconciliation.
The result is a book that will resonate with readers all over the
world.'

Australian Bookseller and Publisher

'*Landscape of Farewell* has a rare level of wisdom and profundity.
Few writers since Joseph Conrad have had so fine an appreciation
of the equivocations of the individual conscience and their
relationship to the long processes of history … [It is] a very human
story, passionately told.'

Australian Book Review

'Miller has crafted a beautifully reflective narrative, navigating
explorations not just of the land but of story and history, of truth-
telling and massacre, and the power and futility of saying sorry.'

Good Reading

Miller's cast of finely drawn, reflective characters enact a powerful
and engaging central story.'   *Adelaide Advertiser*

'… a troubled and powerful look at man's inhumanity to man
… Miller takes [the] set of irrational "truths" buried deep in the
human psyche and makes them the muscle and sinew of his tale:
they become the subliminal engine that drives his story of revenge
and reconciliation to its powerful, uplifting conclusion … In
these moments, *Landscape of Farewell* becomes a rare experience.'

Sydney Morning Herald

Miller's novel is dense with images and ideas. It is clear he is
eminently skilled in giving fictional space to the complex issues
of trauma, guilt, massacre and reconciliation … Miller cannot be
faulted for his willingness to bring complex issues out through the
work of the imagination. That he does this with such skill is to be
celebrated.'   *The Courier Mail*

ALEX MILLER

Landscape *of* Farewell

ALLEN&UNWIN

Also by Alex Miller

Prochownik's Dream
Journey to the Stone Country
Conditions of Faith
The Sitters
The Ancestor Game
The Tivington Nott
Watching the Climbers on the Mountain

For Stephanie
& for my friend Frank Budby, elder of the Barada

This edition published in 2008
First published in 2007

Australian Government This project has been assisted by the Commonwealth
Government through the Australia Council, its arts
funding and advisory board.

Allen & Unwin
83 Alexander Street
Crows Nest NSW 2065
Australia
Phone: (61 2) 8425 0100
Fax: (61 2) 9906 2218
Email: info@allenandunwin.com
Web: www.allenandunwin.com

National Library of Australia
Cataloguing-in-Publication entry:

    Miller, Alex, 1936– .
     Landscape of farewell.
     ISBN 978 1 74175 491 9
     I. Title.
     A823.3

Set in 12/18.5 pt Fairfield Light by Midland Typesetters, Australia
Printed in Australia by McPherson's Printing Group

10 9 8 7 6 5 4 3 2 1

From where rises the high tide of desire, of expectation, of an obsession with sheer being defiant of pain, of the treadmill of enslavement and injustice, of the massacres that are history?

George Steiner

Hamburg
Autumn 2004

1

Agamemnon's edict

On examining my reflection in the hallstand mirror before leaving for the conference that morning, it was not my imminent death nor the poor quality of my paper that concerned me, but that I was in need of a haircut and had once again forgotten to shave. Winifred would have run her fingers along the back of my neck and reproved me, *You need tidying up!* As if I were a neglected room in her house. Winifred never had a house of her own, but in the ideal life of her imagination I am confident she had lived in one. For all the forthrightness of her modern feminist spirit, there was something immovably old-fashioned in Winifred's secret longings and I am sure she saw herself, in this life of her interior fantasies, as the broad-hipped, bosomy mistress of a grand establishment with a vast brood of noisy and unruly children and large dogs. We never talked about it. I just knew it, the way I knew her mood before she came into a room. Could that be where she had gone? Not to nothingness, but teleported to her true home when the summons came? Although I am an unbeliever, I devoutly wished such a blessing on her. For she was a woman who deserved to meet her true—indeed her ideal and imaginary—self one day. Which I cannot say of everyone I meet.

She seemed to stand behind me that morning as I examined my reflection in the mirror, unhappy that her husband, Professor Max Otto, for whom she once possessed ambitions, was not to cut a distinguished figure in front of his colleagues on the occasion of his last appearance before them, but was to be remembered by them at the end as a dishevelled, grieving, defeated old man. But perhaps that is too harsh. I am of average height and a little stooped these days, owing to the persistent pain of a mildly arthritic spine, and my hair, which in my youth was glossy and abundant, floats about at the back of my head like a luminous nimbus. My eyes too have faded—I had not expected this. Once a lustrous amber of great depth and clarity, my eyes are now a pale mud colour and are inclined to water, as if I am forever on the point of weeping—as I should be—or have been peeling onions. And speaking of onions, the skin of my face and neck has become thin and papery, and several of those darkly discoloured patches have appeared on my forehead. I resent this deterioration in my appearance more even than the daily allotment of pain. Until well into my middle years I enjoyed an unblemished complexion, which I no doubt owed to a distant Barbary ancestor. I took this blessing for granted as something that was mine for life, as if it were the unearned due of class or breeding. Absurd vanity! I am able to detect only the faintest remains of that glorious past today. Now I look on a landscape arid and deserted, where once a gay society flourished amid ripening pomegranates and purple grapes, the splash of fountains and cool sounds of laughter from the grove on summer evenings, from where the erotic imploring of the oud aroused our lusts . . .

But I exaggerate. If only it ever had been thus.

I ran my fingers through my ghostly hair, and touched with the forefinger of my right hand a flaky darkness above my left eye, then patted my inside pocket to make certain I had not forgotten my paper and my glasses, and turned from the mirror and went downstairs into the fresh morning. There was the mahogany glint of horse chestnuts littering the footpath and the grass verges. The fine old trees along Schlüterstrasse were clinging to the last of their leaves—as we humans cling to life and to memories beyond their season. It was that brief, charmed period in Hamburg before the cold arrives, when the weather can still be relied upon to be fine, and even reminiscent of summer. It did not seem inappropriate to me that I planned to end my life on such a day. I had written my paper without conviction, obedient to a duty felt more towards the dead than the living. There had been no joy in it. It had been a task imposed on me by the grim moral overseer who rules my life—my conscience, let us say. To claim now that I understood then my true motives for persisting with it would be a lie. Perhaps I persisted because I unconsciously desired a *reason* to persist. Who knows? I cannot truly say what my deeper motives were. I did not know them then and I do not know them now. I had postponed my death in order to write this valedictory paper because my daughter told me Winifred would have wanted me to do it. That was all. I composed it with only the most fleeting moments of pleasure and forgetfulness, and entirely without those surprising instants of inspiration that make intellectual labour worthwhile. Its arguments were concocted from yesterday's leftovers, those stale thoughts out of that mouldering store of notes which I had preserved for thirty years—if preserved is the word for it—in the carton on top of my bookshelves in my study. I dug about in the cold ashes of that youthful folly and *came up* with something for this occasion. I hoped no one would notice how second rate it was, or that if they did notice they would not take offence, but would forgive this faltering of my advanced years and greet it with forbearance and silence.

As I walked down the front steps of our apartment building, little birds flew up at my approach. The publisher's unhappy wife from the apartment below mine, Lydia Erkenbrecht, herself a published poet, had scattered crumbs from her table for them. Or perhaps, more prosaically, not having a family of her own to feed and therefore having few crumbs on her table, the good woman purchased packets of birdseed from the supermarket for this purpose. At any rate, these little street birds were now her family—starlings and sparrows for the most part, with the occasional avuncular pigeon. I had noticed how shamed she was whenever my sudden appearance in the entryway to our building interrupted this pathetic substitution. But she kept on with it, and now the birds had come to rely on her, and she possessed, besides her poetry, if not love, then an object to her persistence rather less pathetic than my own desperate insistence on delivering my last paper to the conference in Aby Warburg's old library.

It was all—all *this*—on account of my wife's death. I had stood at the window of our darkened bedroom that night, looking down into the deserted street, Winifred's photograph clasped to my breast, my hands folded over it as if I were a devout clutching a crucifix to my heart. For me Winifred was still the young woman she had been then. To see her smile was to see the girl in the green scarf standing in the spring sunshine on the Pont Neuf that first morning of our honeymoon. It was a photograph I had taken more than thirty years ago. I looked down from the window into the deserted street, the leaves of the chestnut trees dancing in the wind and making agitated shadows on the glass, as if hands signalled to me, eager for me to understand. Transfixed by helplessness at my loss, I was numb with remembering. Until the moment of her death Winifred was an active woman, her energies youthful and her enthusiasms undimmed. We received no warning. There was no opportunity for us to embrace or to murmur a word of fond farewell. It was the evening of another ordinary day in the new routine of our lives. I had been retired from the university less than a month and she had made arrangements for us to travel to Venice for a holiday the following Monday. She was in the kitchen preparing our evening meal and listening to the new recording of Fauré's *Nocturnes* I had given her. I was sitting on the sofa under the lamp reading a young Harvard professor's *New History of the German People*. The astonishingly able professor was two years younger than our daughter Katriona . . . The hammer blow of Winifred's skull striking the floor tiles drove a spear through my heart—I still feel it. I have no memory of tossing the book aside and crossing the room but was at her side, cradling her head in my arms. In her sightless eyes I saw that she was dead. She was gone. Just like that. In a shocking and mysterious way—which I found strangely humiliating and embarrassing—the body I held in my arms was no longer Winifred. We had been cruelly cheated. I howled to the empty room, begging her to return to me. The silence that greeted my howls, the absence, the nothing that death makes of us, overwhelmed me. I am ashamed to write it, but even in that first moment it was for myself I began to fear. The water for the linguini boiled frantically on the stove above me, spitting tiny arrows of fire onto my neck where I bent over her, Fauré persisting *en mi mineur*. Could I ever be myself again? Panic swept through me and I began to tremble violently. I knew that everything had come to an end.

I stuck it out for a few weeks, perhaps for a month, stumbling around the apartment in a daze, wondering who had brought the flowers and whether I had thanked them, going out to buy eggs and bread and coming home without them, staring emptily at the television hour after hour, an iron band around my chest. Then I made my preparations and telephoned Katriona in London to say goodbye. The whisky and the two small bottles of yellow barbiturate tablets beside the telephone on my night table were a comfort. My good friend Jürgen assured me that in combination they were a painless but certain means for exiting this world of ours. I had never been a whisky drinker. This was to be a new departure for me in more ways than one. A part of me remained detached and interested in the process—the immortal part of me, I suppose it was.

I wept helplessly when my daughter answered the telephone. 'You can't let go of everything just because Mum's no longer there to hold your hand, Dad.' She took me to task as if *I* were *her* child. 'You know Mum would have wanted you to write your paper for the conference this year. Farewells were important to Mum.' She was right of course. I was being selfish. I realised then that the faint ticking I was hearing behind her voice was the click of her computer keyboard—she was multi-tasking. Such was her life. I decided to tell her I was going to kill myself, but changed my mind and instead thanked her for her advice. 'I'm sorry I lost my composure,' I said.

'For heaven's sake, Dad! You're allowed to weep!'

How tired she had sounded herself. Our little Katya no more.

When my paper was announced by the chair, I stood up and approached the rostrum along the centre aisle between the assembled delegates. Do I only fancy it now with the benefit of long reflection, and in the shadow of the events that have since transformed me, or did I experience then a tremulous anticipation, the swift touch of déjà vu, that fleeting breath of a bat's wing in the dark—a premonition, indeed, that my world was about to change once again, a further shift in the cataclysm of my last days, a settling of the debris of my life, which had collapsed around me with such unexpected suddenness?

Was it really so as I walked down that familiar aisle in the grand library of Warburg Haus for the last time, my steps accompanied by the untidy and distracted applause of friends and one-time colleagues? What are we to make of these premonitory experiences? Something shifts, giving in to the pressures that have built for decades in the tectonic plates that support our poor notions of reality, then, suddenly, a whipcrack splits the air about us and we are no longer able to judge our world by the means with which we have habitually judged it. The vista before us, the emotional and psychic vista, I suppose I mean to say, is no longer quite what we have been accustomed to, and we find ourselves strangers among our familiars. It is as if our mother tongue were suddenly gibberish to us, our guidance system scrambled and encoded into an alien snickering for which we possess no cipher. Did I feel it then? Or do I only recollect it now in the retelling of this story—that sudden unsteadiness, the unaccustomed *give* in the ground beneath my feet?

I stood at the lectern and took my paper out of my pocket and unfolded it. I did not see the delegates sitting in rows before me as individuals, but saw a kind of greyness topped, as the Baltic was often topped on summer evenings in my childhood, by little white caps nodding unsteadily on that never-still surface of the sea. I cleared my throat and read into the microphone the title of my paper, 'The Persistence of the Phenomenon of Massacre in Human Society from the Earliest Times to the Present'. I smoothed the pages against the familiar slope of the lectern and began to read. I wished for no more than to be permitted to read my paper and then to slip away quietly, to leave unnoticed and unremarked, having paid my dues to Katriona and to Winifred by doing as I was told. I had always felt more at ease when I did as I was told. I began with a quotation from Homer, the first of the poets—according to Curtius the founding hero, no less, of European literature. Agamemnon, the commander-in-chief of the Greek expedition against Troy, and king of the Mycenaeans, cautions his younger brother, Menelaus, against sparing the life of a high-born Trojan. *We are not going to leave a single one of them alive,* Agamemnon says to his brother, *down to the babies in their mothers' wombs—not even they must live. The whole people must be wiped out of existence, and none be left to think of them and shed a tear . . .*

When I finished reading my paper the applause was scattered and brief, an eager shuffling and murmuring arising at once in the body of the auditorium, almost before the last word was out of my mouth. Homer and massacre were not my subject. I had long ago settled for the intellectual upheavals of the twelfth century—my slim volume on the power achieved by the bishops during that century was the only work of mine to grace the shelves of the university library. The subject of massacre, however, had obsessed me for a time in my youth, but I had found myself unable to make any headway with it owing to my emotional inhibitions, not least of which was a paralysing sense of guilt-by-association with the crimes of my father's generation, and after several false starts I had abandoned the subject and fallen silent. It had remained an unexamined silence throughout my life, and was my principal regret. Perhaps I chose to speak of it at this time because I believed I would not be called upon to defend what I had to say. If that were indeed the case, then I was blind to it and freely admit now that it would have been a dishonourable reason. But enough of these maunderings. The grand project of history, of its discontents, and of the necessity for each generation to rewrite it for themselves, was about to give way to the more immediate matter of the buffet lunch, which the caterers had laid out on trestles in the foyer while I was gibbering on about the obsessions of my youth. Like animals at the zoo that sniff the approach of the keepers with their food, the assembled delegates had grown restless. I stood a moment longer at the lectern.

Why I paused there I cannot say. Perhaps it was a last forlorn need for a sense of completion. Whatever it was, I hesitated to step out of the spotlight. I did not intend staying for the lunch, but was going home to the apartment at once to have done with my life. I was conscious as I stood there that my unblemished suicide stood before me. It was to be the last act of my free will. My noble exit. It was the one thing I might yet do well and not live to regret. As I made to step away from the lectern a young woman seated in the front row to my left rose to her feet and shouted something. Or it sounded like a shout. Her voice was loud and challenging and had about it the expectation almost of unfolding violence. Her wild shout arrested my movement and silenced the assembly. I teetered, neither going nor staying, then righted myself and stayed. The departing delegates turned and looked in her direction for the source of the commotion. Those who had not yet risen broke off their conversations and remained in their seats, and those who had already risen, sensing that something of moment was about to happen, sat down again. And I, caught in the spotlight, stood with my spectacles in one hand while dabbing at my watering eyes with my handkerchief in the other, waiting for what was to come.

She was like a bright, exotic raptor spreading her gorgeous plumage in the midst of the ranks of these drab fowls. Her wild cry evidently called me to account. Once she had established an expectant silence, her voice rode upon it, her words filled with scorn and contempt. She was a woman in command of her audience and was clearly intent upon defending territory. In other words, she was young, intelligent and ambitious. With a touch of annoyance, I realised that I was not going to be permitted to slip away without being required to answer for my shoddy paper. I remained at the lectern—no longer the lecturer, but the accused. I was not so much listening to what she was saying, as fascinated by the spectacle of her performance. She did not stand still but walked back and forth, waving her arms about with vigorous gestures and turning every so often to confront her audience, the loose carmine and green fabrics of her clothing billowing around her as if she danced her meaning for us, the power of her case as much in the brilliance and volume of her movements as in her words.

Settled to her task, her voice took on the largeness

of a bassoon, its tones rich and dark like the tones of her flesh, its volume filling the broad confines of Aby Warburg's stylish library—and evidently penetrating beyond the library to the foyer, for I noticed that the back doors were being held open by curious members of the catering staff, who were looking in at the goings on. The passion of a youthful and righteous conviction vibrated through this young woman and she held us spellbound. I had no doubt that she believed herself to be sounding the last trumpet for me. Her energy, her bright clothes, her large gestures, her determination, her sense that this was her moment, flew like a field of banners about her head. Despite the extravagance of her delivery, however, she proceeded methodically, severe and centred, demolishing my paper point by point, quoting my words precisely with an astonishing facility of recall, her manner haughty and contemptuous. Turned half towards me, she made a careless gesture in my direction—'How can this man presume to speak of massacre,' she asked the enthralled gathering, 'and not speak of my people?' She closed her appeal with a last enveloping, flinging gesture, both arms raised in my direction, as if she cast me and the whole tribe of old men to which I belonged from her presence, and from the presence of all serious intellectual endeavour, forever and ever, amen—or for even longer, if her curse would but endure. For her the wheel of history evidently no longer turned, but had come to a stop at her generation's door. I had witnessed the phenomenon before. Such conviction is always impressive, slightly unnerving, and is usually accompanied by a tendency to an overstatement of the case. As if she suspected herself of just this fault, she laughed. It was a loud, baying, bellow of amusement that bordered on self-caricature— she might almost have shared my thought: *the wheel of history indeed!* She turned abruptly then and stepped down the centre aisle and walked towards the doors, wrapping herself in her colours and not offering me the dignity of a reply—for which last gesture of contempt I was grateful.

Thoroughly entertained, the delegates applauded and watched her progress back along the aisle with delighted approval. A group of students standing by the doors shouted repeated bravos. She was the new Wallenstein and armies of scholars would fall back at her approach. Well, such was the theatre of the moment. Or so it seems to me now as I sit here writing this and doing my best to recollect the details of that day with its dramas and reversals. I am reminded again that it is never simply a

matter of deciding to do something in order to actually do
it. Certain other forces, complementary to our decision
to act, must arise and range themselves alongside us or,
despite our will and determination, we achieve nothing.
However great our resolve, we never do anything alone—
whether for good or ill—even in the matter of our own
death, except of course in the interior ideal world of our
imagination, where our private will is the unhindered
master of ceremonies.

I was still standing at the lectern, clutching my
spectacles and dabbing at my eyes with my damp handkerchief, and no doubt cutting quite as forlorn a figure
as any abandoned bride at the altar. It seemed only right
that this black princess of a barbarous new order should
have arrived at the very moment of my departure. Such
efficiencies of the unexpected must surely be more than
mere coincidence. Is there not in them a conjunction of
historical lines of fracture whose sources are mysterious
and ancient? Could she and I be more than merely actors
on the stage at this fortuitous moment, playing out our
parts as puppets do, without a will or a cause or an effect
to call our own? As I watched her triumphant progress
along the aisle, I saw in her the new commander-in-chief
of the expedition against the old order, her intention none

other than Agamemnon's: *We are not going to leave a single one of them alive!* We—I mean my generation of old men—had failed. Oh, I had known it years ago. I had not doubted our failure for decades. It delighted me now that the baton of the struggle for truth—if we must call it that, and what other word do we possess?—was to pass from my deluded, exhausted and defeated generation into the hands of such as this woman. I would not have been her match even in my youth. There had been none like her then. Just for this moment she had made it seem to us that a moral advancement of our kind might yet be achieved, and we were grateful to her for that. She had made it seem that all was not lost, that things might yet be done that we had dreamed of doing. Humankind, for example, might yet be made good, let us say—there was nothing modest in her style. She was a leader and she had insisted we acknowledge her message. There is a kind of genius of intuition in these things which enables certain individuals to choose their moment well. She had the style of it. And she sowed within each of us—for an hour or two at any rate—new thoughts of liberty and justice. We saw in her the exercise of an incandescent power to preach the word of truth and we were not immune. For goodness' sake, who is? We knew this power—or at least my own generation knew it—to be a dangerous power that is given to a few individuals to exercise briefly over the minds of their fellows. We did not think of danger, however, but happily submitted to her spell. There is a greatly seductive, indeed there is a sensual pleasure in such momentary submission, and we do not resist. No spell, however, no matter how potent, can withstand for long the assault of sceptical reflection. Which is why it is the sceptic, and not the believer, who is in the end our saviour. We go home, we drink a glass or two of wine, we watch the latest news of massacres and famines on the television, and we are restored to sanity, our ecstasy forgotten.

As I stepped down from the lectern for the last time that day, it occurred to me, with a little jolt of pleasure, that there was one decent thing I might yet do before going home and killing myself. I knew at once that Winifred would approve the spirited generosity of the intention. Even though I had just been given my dishonourable discharge, as it were, I smiled at the thought of Winifred's pleasure.

My old colleague and friend, the gifted teacher and amateur flautist Tamás Bartsch, stepped alongside me and took my arm in his—I have known Tamás ever since we were schoolboys together. 'So what is it you find in all this to smile at, dear friend?' he inquired of me solemnly.

'It is the thought of Winifred's pleasure at what I am about to do,' I replied at once, for Tamás and Winifred had greatly admired each other and there was nothing I wished to conceal from this dear man—except, of course, my decision to die within the hour.

'Ah, my poor fellow,' he said and squeezed my arm.

She—I mean the black princess, of course—was standing by the doors at the far side of the library in conversation with the group of admiring students and junior members of staff who had chanted their enthusiastic approval of her performance a few moments before. As Tamás and I came towards them one of the young women indicated my approach to her and she turned and looked at me. When she saw who it was, it was clear from her expression, and in the way she physically set herself to encounter me, that she anticipated a fight. Tamás murmured a desire not to meet her and went on through the door to get himself some lunch. The young woman introduced herself to me as Professor Vita McLelland, from Sydney University.

I offered my hand. She examined my extended hand for a moment as if she thought it might conceal a weapon, then took it in her own. Her clasp was firm, definite and brief, her gaze direct and challenging. She was ready for me. Her manner said, *Bring it on, Professor Otto!*

'Permit me to apologise to you, Professor McLelland,' I said, 'for the poor quality of my paper. You are right, of course, to condemn such shoddiness. It saddens me greatly to have been responsible for your anger. Let me say again, I am sorry. It was not such an end to my career as this that I envisaged when I was a young man of your own age, believe me. Indeed I do not truly understand by what means I have arrived at this shabby state. It is a puzzle to me and has not been by my conscious design, I assure you. I sincerely hope that when you reach the end of your own career, which I am certain will be illustrious, you will do better than I with the question of the succession.'

She looked at me in silence after my little speech. The expression in her beautiful dark eyes was curious, engaged I would say, but disbelieving. She suspected irony, no doubt.

Recalling my beloved father and his state of bewilderment at his death, I said, 'Passing the baton of truth from our own generation to the next has always been a perilous affair. Perhaps especially in my country.' It was an artless expression of my thoughts on this difficult subject, and I feared, even as I said it, that my clumsy expression might give further encouragement to her contempt for me. We may not ourselves have participated directly in massacring our fellow humans—and surely no sane person will hold the children responsible for the murders committed by their fathers—but our troubling sense that we are guilty-by-association with their crimes is surely justified by our knowledge that we are ourselves members of the same murdering species as they. I am a human being first and only second, and by the chance of birth, am I the son of my father and mother. I know myself to be implicated in the guilt of both my species and my parents, for it is to these categories of being, and to these only, that I own a sense of membership.

I was concerned that my apology might have sounded pompous to her, for it had been delivered in the very voice of the old order, which she was determined to silence. She did not relax but remained on her guard, evidently anticipating some trickery on my part. 'Goodbye, Professor McLelland,' I said and I smiled to see a doubt still for an instant the fierce and uneasy lights that flickered within the depths of her dark eyes. 'May I wish you good fortune in the struggle.' I inclined my head to her, an indulgence in an old-fashioned courtesy more familiar to my father's generation than to my own. It was a private, and somewhat symbolic, gesture of farewell, however, to life and to a generation, and perhaps to my father's hopes for me. Yes, even that. It was a homage to the ghosts of my own fallen heroes, to those men—and they had all been men—whose books in my youth had seemed destined to stand forever as imperishable landmarks in the epic story of a Europe that had, since then, ceased to exist, their names unknown to this woman's generation, their works no longer valued or read. New histories have arisen since then. In our youth it is only the histories we write ourselves that seem to us to be just and true. As we grow old ourselves, however, our youthful certainties begin to fail us, just as our bodies do, and we see at last that we have been wrong to have believed as we have believed and that truth has no permanence but is a shifting thing.

I turned aside and walked through the lunching crowd. I pushed the doors open and walked down the steps, leaving the grand old library of Aby Warburg behind me. Professor Vita McLelland from Sydney University was the future. I was glad I had met her face to face. I was glad, too, to have held her hand and to have seen how she had at the last moment looked searchingly into my eyes and been affected by the heartfelt sincerity of my apology. I was glad for my father's memory, for his *sake*, indeed—for he still lived in my heart—that mine had not, after all, been a dishonourable end. On my way to my death I was feeling a rather silly optimism for the future of humankind, my judgment rattled, no doubt by the emotion of the moment, and my senses a little dizzy with the wonder of Professor Vita McLelland's glorious youth. How wonderful it would have been to live again that grand illusion.

2

The appointment

Outside the library the street was strangely still and deserted, the big houses of the wealthy burghers silent and shuttered. A sense of impending action confronted me along the avenue of great trees—I might have stepped onto the set of a film between takes. Then I saw the van, a nasty amateurish green, obviously repainted hurriedly in a back alley only the night before. It crouched at the kerb, low and menacing. At any moment its doors would burst open and the assassins tumble out shouting obscenities and firing their automatic weapons.

Her shout close behind startled me and as I spun around I tripped on an uneven paving stone. She grasped me strongly by my upper arm and dragged me upright against her. 'You can't get away from me that easily, Professor Otto!' She laughed, her face so close to mine I caught the sweet nutty tang of her breath. She did not relinquish my arm but held onto me, as if she expected me to fall to the ground without her support. She searched my eyes with such a close and intimate inspection of their contents that she might have suspected me of secreting within myself some precious stolen possession of her own. Her scrutiny was disconcerting and faintly exciting, exposing me to something against which I had no defence and arousing in me the rare and rather delightful delusion of erotic expectation—I might have found myself suddenly naked and alone with her on the street. She laughed at my confusion and, apparently reassured by what she had seen within, relaxed her close examination and slipped her arm comfortably through mine, pressing it to her fleshy side.

'You can shout me a drink before you go. I want to hear that apology of yours in triplicate,' she said. 'I've never had one of those from any of you guys before.' With sudden impatience she set off, hauling me along with her. 'I feel as if I'm beginning to smell of old books in those places,' she said. Gripping my arm with a confidence that astounded me, she flung a contemptuous look over her shoulder at Warburg Haus and, with a crude vehemence that I found a little shocking, she announced loudly to the empty street, 'God, don't you just *hate* those old libraries.'

We had gone quite a little way before I gathered myself sufficiently to respond to her. 'Erich Auerbach,' I gasped—I was short of breath from a combination of the suddenness of the action and the sheer physical awe she inspired in me. 'Auerbach,' I said breathlessly, 'claimed he would never have written his great book if he had had access to the specialised libraries of Europe.'

'I know just how he felt,' she said.

I held back—almost skidding my heels against her momentum, becoming a stubborn mule and refusing to go further, and eventually forcing her to slacken her pace.

She stopped and frowned at me. 'What's up, Professor?'

I drew breath. 'I should like very much to buy you a drink, Professor McLelland,' I said. 'Indeed nothing would give me greater pleasure, but unfortunately I have an urgent appointment.' She looked so downcast at this that I at once regretted it—the fierce flame of her passion was evidently fragile and could be doused in a moment.

'Urgent?' she queried me doubtfully. 'And it's Vita. Never mind the *professor*.' She frowned at me, distrustful. 'What is it then, a deadline?'

'Well, yes, that is exactly what it is.' It is strange how often our language inveigles us into pronouncing the literal truth when our intention is to deceive.

'You're not being very convincing. It's your wife, isn't it?' With a sudden outburst of exasperation—and once again she seemed to interrogate not me but the world at large—she said, 'Why has every man I ever meet got a wife waiting at home for him?'

I said, 'My wife is dead.'

She closed her eyes. 'Oh God!' She opened her eyes and looked at me beseechingly. 'I'm so sorry. I'm truly sorry. I've done it again. Please forgive me. I go charging in. I tell myself, *Don't do it, Vita!* Then I do it. I'm always bullying people before I know half their story.' She pressed my arm to her side and asked with gentle concern, 'Will you please forgive me? Can I ask you how long it has been?'

'A few months only.'

'You poor man. You must miss her terribly.'

'Yes, I do.' I thought I might weep.

'Please tell me you forgive me, or I shall have to kill

myself.' She was at once playful again; the pretty child twisting her beloved daddy's feelings around her little finger. I found it impossible to resist gazing into the inviting ocean of Vita McLelland's generous dark eyes— deep pools of emotion, they were, in which thoughts and ideas and uncertainties flashed and darted about in excited shoals. Such abundance, so long absent from my own interior life, mesmerised me. I hoped she would not notice how distracted I was by her.

'There is nothing for me to forgive,' I said. 'How could you have known?'

The assured familiarity with which she held my arm throughout this exchange was a strangely compelling comfort to me, and I hoped she would not soon let me go. She might have laid claim to me. Although she was so much younger than I, there was something motherly and protective in the way she held me. I sensed an almost familial appeal in this direct, unabashed intimacy; a need to offer comfort where comfort was needed. Or perhaps she appealed for my understanding, for my protection, for my friendship? I was not sure. Was she lonely? Not without a circle of friends and intimates, I mean, but deeply lonely, a solitary who would cling to a stranger briefly, a sudden flare of recognition and companionship, then emptiness, nothing, the awful dragging void of melancholy. Could a visionary such as she—a leader, no doubt, among her people—ever be other than alone? Were not such fierce people always alone? Perhaps it was only what I wanted to believe of her.

'Now *you've* said sorry to me and *I've* said sorry to you,' she said. 'Hey, Max! Come on!' She let go of me and flung open her arms so that her clothes bloomed suddenly about her. 'You and I have got to get past this stage of trying to out-apologise each other.'

We both laughed.

'There, we're even now,' she said and she tucked my arm against her side again—where she and I evidently felt it was most right for it to be. '*I'll* buy *you* a drink. And don't tell me you haven't got time for just the one before your appointment. Be late for once.' She stood still and examined me. 'I've never struck one like you. You old blokes defend your work viciously to the last breath in your bodies. You never, *never* say sorry. Hey, folks, I got it wrong. I'm sorry. No. Never that. I've never heard it. You're a rare bird, Max. What do people around here think of you? I'll bet you've got a few of them puzzled. You're not getting rid of me until we've had a tête-à-tête.'

She adjusted my arm against her side and we set

off down the street. She was more sedate now in her pace, more certain, I suppose, that she had secured a companion for the next hour or two. 'So where's the pub?' she said. 'Point me at it.'

By the way, I am not making any of this up. It all happened to me only a little over a year ago, just as I am reporting it here. I loathe books that are made up, as if life is not enough.

We were sitting across from each other at a table in the recess of a window, the remains of our meal still on the table. I had never been inside the bar but had often passed it on my way to the railway station. Vita was talking, the long slender fingers of her left hand played with her glass—her wedding hand, she said, without a ring, holding it up, 'See?' And she smiled her vulnerable, sad smile, not the fierce smile of the warrior princess. Though her hand had once carried the precious ornament for a little while, she said. I watched her. She had lovely hands. She played with her glass, her head on one side, considering—what? Her voice was loud and penetrating at first, and the young man who had brought our meal had looked across at her and listened, and she had given him to understand that she knew he was listening to her and that she did not care. As the bar filled up with drinkers her voice drew back and became softer and more private.

I noticed, suddenly, that my wineglass was empty again. The last time I had looked it had been full. I wondered, for an instant, who could have emptied it. Beyond the window, outside in the street, it was already dark. The bar was crowded now with young people and was noisy with their laughter and shouting. Beneath the clamour of their voices their tribal music maintained a steady beat. I had stopped trying to follow what Vita was saying some time ago and was attending to the throbbing of the music, which to my surprise I found calming and conducive to a kind of inner and solitary melancholy. I should have been dead by now, or at least drifting towards that state on the irresistible currents of an ever-deepening stupor.

The steady throb of the music was precisely the sound of my uncle's old single-cylinder tractor. An enormous green monster, it was—I wonder why my monsters are always green? It is a cliché of my generation, I suppose, to paint our fears green, whereas nowadays it is hope that greens the world. The monster was mounted on iron wheels. As a child I had more than half-believed it to be an ancient man who had been transformed into a giant machine by my uncle, who I knew to be in possession of unearthly powers. From the open window of my upstairs bedroom in the farmhouse, I listened to the tractor all day, spellbound by the drumbeat of its great heart, the tremorous thud of its powerful pump vibrating the fabric of the house, sounding in my own heart images of a distant enchanted reality. I could see it, that enchanted place: there were dark woods fringed by wide deserts, the faintly apprehended party of mounted figures in the distance, going I knew not whither, to what terrible destination beyond the far horizon no living man could know. Indeed the anguished heartbeat of the ancient man imprisoned within the iron machine inspired my first true daydream of another life. It was a life, this imaginary one, that I knew I would never quite reach or master, but it was ever thereafter the emblem of my inner yearning. Though outwardly I have changed quite beyond recognition from my boyhood self, inwardly little has changed. I still see that mysterious band of horsemen—if that is what they are—who ride together in silent company towards the end of time.

I was filled with anxiety and excitement when my uncle started the tractor in the yard in the frosty morning, exploding with a confident blow of his hammer a shotgun cartridge in the small cylinder embedded within the blunt nose of the tractor—the casing of this cartridge was always a hopeful blue, instead of the blood red of the shells with which he shot the crows and foxes. That confident hammer blow convinced me he was a great demon in his own world. The violence of the explosion in the silence of the winter morning made me flinch and woke the ancient man from the cold night of his sleep, his deep throbbing groan shuddering in my own chest as he bent his iron frame to the labour of his enslavement. During the long winter months of that year, alone with my uncle on the farm and without the reassuring presence of my mother and father, I inhabited a place of beguiling strangeness. The cold metallic smell of the ploughed earth opened by the sleek plough was for me like the opened belly of a dead horse I had come upon one day when I was walking home, the massive innards scattered about the great carcass by the crows, as though for modesty's sake a passer-by had thrown over it a bright patchwork shawl.

There had been scarcely a pause in Vita's flow of words since we left the library—marching arm in arm beneath the chestnut trees along pompous Heilwigstrasse. She had been telling me her troubles, which were many and complex, involving either members of her family or colleagues at her university, or her repeated failure to attract the right man.

I saw she was a little drunk. I was a little drunk myself. I did not mind at all.

She reached across the table and punched me on the arm. 'Hey, Max! I've forgotten what I was going to say!'

I lifted my shoulders and smiled. 'Then say something else.'

She frowned, concentrating. 'What was I talking about?'

'You were telling me about your Uncle Dougald.'

'You and Uncle Dougald would get on.'

I imagined a tall, broad-shouldered, square-jawed Scot, McLelland of McLelland, weather-beaten and fierce, a true colonial pioneer, axe at rest on the stump of the great gum tree he has just felled, frowning belligerently at the intrusion of the camera, behind him his half-built shack, a scene located somewhere in the timbered wilds of Australia, a woman and a child looking on, helpless if this man's arm should falter. It was an image not from my own mind this, but drawn from my old storybooks of the New World.

Behind Vita, beyond the window, the rain glistened on

the iron railings and the headlights of cars passed along the street. 'You're young to be a professor,' I said.

'I'll be forty-one at Christmas.'

I was surprised. 'I thought you were about twenty-seven.'

'I'm immature, I know. Tell me about it!'

I began at once to see her differently.

'Don't stare,' she said. 'It's rude.'

I apologised. She laughed and punched my arm again, a little harder this time. Perhaps she wished to wake me from old age. I had not sat in a bar with a companion for many years. Not since I was a student. Winifred and I had never sat in a bar together. I believed, however, that Winifred would not have objected had she been able to see me drinking with Vita in this bar next to the Kellinghusenstrasse railway station, whose arcades are, at night, a favourite beat for the sad-eyed young women who dedicate their tender lives to prostitution. The thought of the young girls, the sight of their sad-eyed countenances, always made me think of our little Katya. Those tragic young women. Lost to life. Where were their mothers and fathers? Why did they not come and take their little girls home? I could not remember if I had told Vita about our daughter.

'Have I told you about Katya?' I said. My glass, I noticed, was full again. I reached for it and drank the dark red wine—it had the taste of aluminium.

At my question, she looked around the bar with sudden interest. 'This place is jumping,' she said. She looked at me. 'Katya? She's your daughter? What a beautiful name for a little girl.' She said this as if she referred to a girl known only to herself, an imaginary girl who lived somewhere far away.

'Yes. She has changed her name to Katriona and has become English.'

She waved a hand at me. 'So don't tell me, I already know, she's happily married. To a brain surgeon.'

'She is married to a teacher. They have two children.'

'So let's go and see your grandchildren.'

'Katya lives in London.'

'Is she happy?' she asked in a bored voice.

'I don't know.'

'You should call her Katriona. That's who she wants to be. Me? I'm ready and waiting for the first big black Murri prince who comes along and tries his luck.' She examined me, a look of faint irritation in her eyes suddenly. 'You haven't said a word about yourself all night. You don't know if your own daughter is happy or not. That's all

I know about you. You should go over there and spend time with your grandchildren. They won't know their grandad and one day soon they'll want to know why. Family is family, Max.'

'I think it's quite late,' I said. I consulted my watch.

She looked startled. 'Hey, don't you go abandoning me. Jesus, Max! Don't you even think of it!'

I was shocked by her fear of being abandoned by me late at night on the streets of Hamburg. 'Of course I shan't abandon you. How could you think such a thing? I shall see you to your hotel. This is my city, Vita.'

She pouted, like a child who has been chastised. Then she brightened, a mischievous look coming into her enormous dark eyes. 'You're pissed, Max.' She laughed. 'And, hey!' She pointed a finger at me as if she had achieved an important advantage. 'I made you miss your appointment! I bet they gave you up for dead hours ago.'

'I had no appointment,' I said.

'You lied? You bastard!' She cursed me mildly and with amused surprise, as if she were delighted to discover me capable of such paltry deceit. She sniggered, 'You didn't want to be seen walking down the street with a black lady on your arm.'

'That is not true, Vita,' I said seriously. I was acutely

sensitive to the offence of her suggestion, even though she made the charge playfully.

But she was not listening to me. She cast about her as if she had mislaid something, fidgeting and nervous suddenly, reaching for her coat, searching in her bag then snapping it closed, gathering the loose folds of her elaborate clothing about her; readying herself for flight. She looked up at me, her gaze distracted. 'So what are we going to do? They're closing this place.'

It was true. The young man who had been serving us was collecting glasses and wishing his customers goodnight. Vita watched me. She was no longer the haughty black princess of the barbarous new order, but was just another lonely woman in a bar with a stranger at closing time.

I heard myself say, 'I have a bottle of whisky at home.'

3

Tête-à-tête

I closed the door to the apartment softly behind us and switched on the hall light. What would the publisher's unhappy wife, the poet Lydia Erkenbrecht, lying awake in her lonely bed, make of this tête-à-tête that is taking place in the apartment above her head? *So he is going to behave just as he pleases now, and she only a month or two in her grave.* The mother of the little birds, into whose defenceless ears she murmurs her bitter discontents.

I followed Vita along the hall and into the sitting room. She walked across the rug and stood admiring Winifred's Biedermeier cabinet. It was our only antique piece and had belonged to Winifred's grandmother. I stood by the hall door watching Vita trail her fingers over the polished surface of the cabinet. The intricate marquetry and honey-coloured wood of the old piece had been the symbolic spiritual reliquary of Winifred's ancestral home.

Vita turned and looked back at me. 'How beautiful this is,' she said, not sharing her wonder with me, but thinking of something remote and private. She turned back to the cabinet and touched it again. 'It's from another world.'

'Yes,' I said, responding to the fiction that it was me she had addressed. 'You are right. It is all that is left of the elaborate furnishings of a once-grand Viennese household.' The household, indeed, of which Winifred had secretly dreamed herself the exemplary big-bosomed, broad-hipped chatelaine, a place she had never visited but had heard about from her own mother. It was her legendary house of the ancestors, and had been destroyed during the war, like so much else ancestral—but for the miraculous survival of this cabinet, which had come down to her unscratched, as if it were a sign to her direct from her grandmother's Vienna. The precious piece had been Winifred's link to all that mattered to her in her past, all that she had believed to have once been good and decent—her nostalgia for an innocent ancestral past that had never really existed. I said, 'Your admiration would have pleased Winifred. That cabinet meant a lot to my wife.'

She let her hand fall to her side and murmured something, losing interest. She turned and walked the few paces to the couch under the window and dropped heavily onto it. She arranged herself where I had been sitting reading on the evening Winifred was struck down. A tremor passed through me to see her seated there.

She considered me, frowning. 'What?' she asked irritably.

She was pouting, and looked incredibly young suddenly, a discontented teenager. She is achingly tired, I thought, and is wishing she had not agreed to come here but had got into a taxi outside the bar and said her farewells and gone straight back to her hotel. Her stream of words and goodwill had failed her. I thought of offering to call her a taxi, but hesitated to do so. If she accepted my offer, the moment I waved her goodbye I would be alone with my bottle of whisky and my pills, and I would have to decide whether to go through with my planned suicide. I did not want to be alone in the apartment confronting that question. The thought of it frightened me. I wondered how I might convince Vita to stay the night. I said, 'Would you like to see the rest of the apartment? My study is rather fine.'

She closed her eyes and shook her head slowly from side to side, as if the idea of it made her feel ill.

'I'll get the whisky then,' I said. I knew, suddenly, that I was not going to kill myself. It was not even an issue. I felt relief and disappointment in almost equal measure at this realisation. I was confronting once again the man I might have been and the man I really was. There was to be no heroic order of absolution. I should have known it. Winifred would have understood my suicide, and might even have admired me for it. But this retreat with a young woman she would not admire.

When I came out of the bedroom with the bottle of whisky Vita still had her eyes closed and was even more deeply scrunched into the corner of the couch, her legs folded under her. She was hugging a cushion to her breasts, as if she was in need of warmth, or was shielding herself. She might have been waiting for someone for hours and they had not turned up and she had given up hope of seeing them ever again but could not rouse herself sufficiently to get up and leave. I touched her shoulder and she opened her eyes and glared at me. She released the cushion with one hand and took the glass of whisky from me. She sipped the neat liquor, making a face and watching me narrowly, clutching the glass close to her chin.

'So what did your dad do during the war, Max?' she said and laughed. 'You'd better tell me and get it over with.' She laughed again and leaned forward to set the glass on the coffee table, then sank back into the couch. Nursing the cushion at her breasts once again, she closed her eyes. 'Just talk,' she commanded. 'Say anything.'

I stood looking down at her. The little dream of gentle companionship that she and I had celebrated together in the bar had quite vanished now, and might never have been. What was I to say for myself? I was born in central Europe in 1936 and my early years were fashioned by the war. My *life* was fashioned by the war. The war was something that had happened to this young woman's grandparents, in a past as remote as Winifred's grandmother's Vienna had been for her. A past, in other words, about which it was possible to be nostalgic. The war was not something I could ever be nostalgic about. The war had trapped my generation in an iron cage of remorse and silence. 'I remember the war vividly,' I said.

Vita opened her eyes and looked up at me. 'You don't

have to talk about the war,' she said. 'I didn't mean it. I was joking. It's an Australian joke. Okay? Don't be so earnest, Max, for God's sake.'

'I don't mind,' I said. 'I'd quite like to talk about the war with you. I feel as if I could.' She had closed her eyes again. Was I about to become an old bore who had drunk too much wine and would insist on unloading his past onto this poor girl? 'The war determined my life.' She did not respond. 'It's late,' I said. Any minute now she would open her eyes and gather herself and ask me to call a taxi for her. Most of the whisky was still in the bottle.

I was suddenly deeply tired. My limbs, my arms and legs, my neck even, were weighted with sandbags, and my lungs were unable to extract sufficient oxygen from the air. I sat heavily in the armchair opposite her and took a gulp of whisky—the whisky which had been meant to set me on my way. After a moment she began to snore.

'So,' I heard myself murmur, 'you are not dead then?' Perhaps I *was* dead. It was difficult to tell. Had I blinked and missed the trip across the border? Had it all been managed so smoothly that I had not felt a thing— something like an open-heart operation? After all, almost anything can be done these days and it is difficult to know what state we are really in. Here I was, back in the apartment, with a beautiful young black woman asleep on our couch where I had sat myself that fatal evening. And Vita *was* beautiful. Very beautiful. There is no point being coy about it. I sat there sipping the whisky admiring her beauty. She was a meteor that had arrived out of the sky and struck me a glancing blow. Soon she would be on her way again, slightly deflected in her own course by this fleeting contact with the old professor in Hamburg. But where would I be?

She did not snore evenly but snuffled and jerked about. It was delightful. Winifred had also snored. Hers had been a regular, deep, throbbing snore originating like the note of a trombone deep in the back of her throat, or even in her diaphragm. It was a reliable sound and I had found it soothing and had for years happily gone off to sleep to it. Winifred's snoring had been my lullaby. Vita looked older than her forty-one years now. The teenager was gone. Older? No, not older. Perhaps ageless would be a more accurate way of putting it. Altered, at any rate. Yes, she was altered. Not a meteor after all but a storm-tossed bird from a remote tropical island come to rest at last after a long and hazardous migration, wrapped in the soiled and broken fabric of her gaudy wings. But no, that will not do either. Vita was far too voluptuously constructed to be a bird. Even in this world in which the exotic has become the everyday, Vita was exotic. I am sure she would be pleased to hear me say it. The impression was not accidental, but was the result of a considered strategy. Sitting there on my couch, she was not of my world, and she did not wish to be mistaken as being of it. She did not belong in Hamburg. I do not mean that she was unwelcome in Hamburg. On the contrary. We may make strangers welcome and even love them and take them into our homes and into our hearts, but that does not make them belong. To belong is something else. Belonging, home, the meaning of such things is not to be settled through argument and the presentation of evidence, or even facts. Such things are enigmas and their truth is not rational but is poetic, their uncertainties not resolvable into facts and proofs. Indeed the less that is decided about such things in public life the better it will be for all of us.

Of course I was still thinking about her question: *what did your dad do during the war?* How could I not think about it? I had been meditating on the question all my life. Although my parents were not devout Christians, my mother and my sister and I knelt beside my mother's bed every night throughout the war and prayed to God to bring my father home safely to us from the front. I retain an image among my collection of childhood images; it is of the three of us in the dim lamplight of my mother's bedroom, kneeling side by side, our hands clasped, our heads bent, our eyes firmly closed against our doubts. That was us, the devotional family. There were even moments in those days when I believed in God's mercy. It was a wonderful feeling. It was faith, I suppose. Childhood faith. For a time my prayers went straight to heaven. Later, something began to block them and they ceased to get through to Him. All my early experiences were of the war. I knew little else until I was nine. My world until that age consisted principally of God, death and an awful silence. If I did not speak about those things all the time later in my life, it was not because they were not continuously murmuring their lament to me, but because I was a member of a strict monastic order that required from its adherents a vow of silence. I am not speaking literally, of course.

When I was a boy I longed to know my father was an honourable soldier. What can honour signify to us today? What does it mean? Honour is like faith, surely. It is something from our childhood. A myth our ancestors needed but which as grown-ups we are content to do without. Honour is as much a part of history as muzzle loaders. These days it is something that mafia capos die for in Hollywood films. Honour is part of our nostalgia for a past that was never real, but which has its imaginary existence only in such places as Winifred's calm, serene, civilised, ancestral Vienna. What a place! What a fairy tale! We are enjoined somewhere by some authority or other—it is probably in one of the Gospels—*Honour thy father and thy mother*. I did. I loved my father and mother. Winifred and I knew we could never say anything that would change the way things had been for our parents' generation. It was too vast to deal with. Too awful. Without ever making a pact, we nevertheless permitted each other to keep silent about it. We expected each other not to speak of it. We respected our fathers and mothers by taking a vow of silence. It was a mistake, no doubt. It was fear and weakness that made us do it. We felt ourselves to be inadequate to the history they had lived . . .

I saw, suddenly, that Vita was watching me and knew I had been murmuring my thoughts aloud.

'There's nothing I can't ask my dad,' she said.

I refreshed her glass and my own. 'A German could never have asked me that question,' I said. 'Not even as a joke. What did your father do in the war is not a question

a stranger of your generation could ever ask a man of my
generation in this country.'

She blinked and sniffed and drew herself together.
'If you'd really loved your father and he'd loved you, you
would have been able to ask him anything.'

I took a mouthful of the whisky and swallowed it.
It had ceased to have a taste. 'It was *because* I loved
my father that I could not ask him such a thing.' The
possibility that my father had not been a good and decent
soldier but had exercised some other terrible duty had
been too hideous to ever risk such a question.

I got up to stand at the window. The streetlights
glittered through the shifting web of the chestnut trees.
It was raining. A young couple was walking home along
the other side of the street. They were not hurrying but
were sauntering, as if the sun were shining on them.
He was holding his coat over their heads. She leaned
against him, her arm through his, her head resting on
his shoulder. Surely he was telling her a story about their
future together? Behind them the dome of the university
library was silvery with the rain, as if it were the dome
of an oriental mosque. Winifred and I often stood at the
window with our arms around each other, looking out at
the street before going to bed.

'After the war was over,' I said, 'we held our breath in case anyone ever dared ask such a question as the one you asked me. It sounds a simple thing to you, but to me, to all of us, it was impossibly difficult. We just wanted to be viewed as human beings again. To be ordinary people. To be part of life and not have to apologise for being the children of our fathers. I've felt all my life that I've had to apologise for my existence. I've always known myself to have been on the wrong side. You might think that has been a small price to pay. And of course it has been. It was never that I didn't *want* to ask my father what he did during the war. I couldn't ask him.' I did not turn around to see if she was listening to me. The young man and the girl were gone now and the street was deserted.

'When he was home with us again after the war, in the evening, at the table doing my homework, I watched my father reading the newspaper by the fireside and I often imagined myself asking him, *Dad, what did you really do in the war?* But I could never say it out loud. In this little play of mine, my father responded to my question without the least sign of tension. *Why, my son, I was the captain of a company of infantrymen. They were fine soldiers, a loyal company, and we behaved as good men do even in the terrible circumstances of war.* After this reassurance, in my little play, we all breathed freely. That is what I wanted. To breathe freely. That is all. To know that our lives were built on something morally sound and decent and that the touch of a single question would not drop me and my entire family into the void. But it was an impossible dream. I knew, we all knew, that we had forfeited the right to such a dream. That perhaps we had forfeited it forever.

'After a while my father felt me watching him and he looked up from his newspaper and asked me if I needed help with a maths problem. He was an engineer by profession. I let him help me, even though I did not find maths difficult and knew the answer to the problem in front of me. After he helped me he went back to his newspaper, and the little circle of our family remained closed, the seal in place. My mother looked across at me with gratitude, then she went on with her sewing; or she got up and gave the fire a poke and suggested we have a cup of hot chocolate before going to bed. Or, sometimes, she came over to me and stood behind my chair and rested her hands on my shoulders, and she looked over my homework and in her quiet voice she congratulated me, as if it was the quality of my work that pleased her. But really it was that I had respected our secret vow of silence.'

I realised I could hear the faint tinkling through the wall of Signore Ciciriello playing Bach on his beloved clavichord. I imagined the light around him thronged with the dancing figures of the old Italian master's dreams. He was far older than I, nearly a quarter-century older, and his memories of war were more vivid than mine. I turned from the window.

Vita was watching me. She was holding the rim of her glass against her chin. 'Do you hear it?' I asked, entranced—I am always more responsive to Bach's voice when I hear him muted by distance, as if I *overhear* him, receiving him not as something from my own world, but as if he leaks through to me from another, purer place of far deeper enchantment than this world can ever be.

'I am sorry,' I said, 'that I never asked my father the question. I regret it. At the time of his death I congratulated myself on allowing him to die peacefully. He was holding my hand when he died. He smiled at me. We kept the faith of our silence to the end. We learned something about deep silence. But it was not the right thing to do. I still regret it. Looking back I see that to have insisted on knowing the truth was the least I might have done, no matter what the consequences. But I lacked the courage.'

She sat watching me for some time, saying nothing, her expression sober and thoughtful. She looked tired and strangely familiar, as if we had known each other for years instead of hours.

I said, 'I have never told anyone this before.'

'Your father must have known the question of his guilt or innocence was preying on your mind. It was cruel of him to remain silent. Why didn't he speak to you? It wasn't up to you. You were only a little boy then. It was up to him too. If he loved you, he should have reassured you. When he felt you watching him in the evening like that, he must have guessed what was really on your mind. Your mother too, she knew it wasn't your homework. They must have both known. And what about your sister? Didn't you talk about these things with her? Where was she all this time?'

'You don't understand,' I said. 'My father had survived the war. For men of his generation who survived there was no possibility of innocence. The pressure to remain silent was enormous, it was irresistible. Later, I turned my back on the present and looked away from the problems of my own times and the times of my parents and I lost myself in the endless beauties of the documents of the twelfth century. After the war it was no longer possible to believe in ourselves. There was an innocence in the remote past that we could never have in our own time. I could not face the truth of what we had done. No one could. It was impossible to face it. No matter how much we say about these things, no matter how truthful we are, no matter how ruthlessly we expose the terrible detail of those events, there will always remain something we cannot say. There will always be something left in the silence.'

'What will it be?' she asked.

'We have no word for it.'

She sat there scrunched into herself, watching me. I could feel her trying to make up her mind, trying to decide whether she was to like or to dislike me. I very much wanted her to approve of me. I waited, with a considerable sense of unease, for her verdict.

She said, 'It's not a sin to have regrets, Max. It's only a sin to deny having them so we don't have to do anything about them.' She fell silent then, thinking again. 'Why you didn't ask your questions and why you didn't write your book on massacre is probably a good deal more important and interesting than what would have been in such a book if you *had* written it.' She set her empty glass heavily on the table and heaved herself to the edge of the couch. 'I'm right. I know I'm right. So no more bullshit. I hate bullshit. Get me a cab. It's time I went home.'

'You can sleep here,' I said. 'You can sleep in our old bed. I have a day bed in my study.' She flopped back and closed her eyes. I stood looking down at her. After a minute she opened her eyes.

'What is it now?' she asked suspiciously. I must have been looking at her strangely. Before the night was over I wanted her to know the true significance for me of our meeting. In the morning it would be too late. In the morning we would be sober and it would no longer be possible for us to be candid with each other. 'Before I met you today,' I said, 'I was planning to kill myself.'

'Jesus!' It was an exclamation of relief. 'I thought you were going to ask me to sleep with you!' She laughed, her laughter wild and filled with fatigue. She struggled into a sitting position and made an impatient, sweeping gesture at me with her hand. 'So what? I've been going to kill myself heaps of times. Who hasn't?'

'I was serious.'

'We're always serious when we're going to kill ourselves.' She stood up, tugging impatiently at the elaborate layers of her clothes, pulling her skirts around and reaching behind her and jerking the various elements of her complicated blouse into position. 'God I hate clothes!' She stopped fiddling and turned to me. 'The time to kill ourselves is after we've paid our debts, not before. Where's this bed you're talking about? Why do I always get drunk? Why can't I do this for once without getting drunk?'

4

The promise

We picked up her bags from the hotel and drove in my old Peugeot along Grindelallee towards the airport. Neither of us had a lot to say. It was raining and the roads were black and slippery. The morning traffic seemed to be particularly aggressive and impatient. I am not confident of my driving skills and was intimidated by the closeness of the other cars. I was very anxious that I might find myself in the wrong lane and would miss the turnoff to the airport. Vita was slumped in the seat beside me, her mood as dark and gloomy as the day. We were both suffering from hangovers and a lack of sleep. I have never liked driving and have avoided doing it as much as possible. Winifred was our driver. More than twenty years ago, when the Peugeot was new, she drove as fast as the car would go along the route to Lübeck and Travemünde, laughing and talking and looking around at Katya in the back, and pointing out interesting features of the scenery along the way. Winifred inspired confidence. I never felt nervous with her behind the wheel. And she never had an accident. Not even a small one. She was an exceptional woman.

This morning, with Vita sitting beside me, I was feeling a little panicked and was finding it a challenge to keep the Peugeot in the tiny space left to me by the other cars. It did not help my concentration that I was also grimly aware that in an hour or two I would be back in the apartment on my own, facing the problem of what to do with the remainder of my life now that I had pardoned myself from the death penalty. I did not fancy the idea of writing poetry, or making friends with the birds. We were waiting at a crossing for the lights to change to green and I was watching an old man cross in front of us. He did not have an umbrella and walked through the rain unaware that he was getting soaked, or beyond caring. The shoulders of his overcoat were blackly sodden. As he tottered forward, his head nodded and his mouth gaped, his watery eyes staring before him as if something terrifying lay in his path. His life, I suppose it was, that he contemplated. The miserable remnant of it that remained to him. In truth he was probably little older than I.

The sight of him appalled me and I clamped my jaw shut and steadied my head on my neck. What was to be done? The dismay on the faces of the old tells its own story. Their world is not our world. It is old age, not the past, that is a foreign country. We observe its inhabitants all our lives, not as if we are looking at ourselves in the future, but as if we are observing another species than our own. How often do we hear the phrase, *to grow old gracefully*, as if this were an essential virtue of our humanity? But how is such grace to be achieved? Old age is not a graceful thing. Yesterday morning the idea of my death did not trouble me, but to think of entering this last stage of life alone, this final solitary advance—or retreat, rather . . . Well, I did not wish to think about it. It made me angry that I had been reminded of it.

I hated the old man for that moment, and when the lights changed to green I pushed down hard on the accelerator with my foot. The bald rear tyres of our old '83 Peugeot hissed on the wet road and for a chilling instant I lost control. I murmured an apology, but Vita seemed not to have noticed the car's sickening lurch. I wondered what she was thinking. At her hotel earlier I had waited in the lobby while she went to her room and changed out of the elaborate costume she had worn for her performance the previous day, which by then was looking wilted and unconvincing. She soon reappeared in a smart black business suit, a pale scarf at her throat. The scarf was a rather subtle and expensive faded pink and it cast a faint reflection of its warmth onto her features, as if she were gently bathed in an unearthly glow. Not only I, but everyone in the hotel lobby, women as well as men, turned to watch her progress towards me across the carpet. Even in a simple black suit, Vita was an event.

She had been silent ever since we left the hotel car park, but after I accelerated away from the doddering apparition she roused herself. She looked straight ahead through the windscreen at the rain sheeting across the road. 'You owe a debt to Winifred,' she said, evidently voicing the conclusion of a private meditation of some duration. She might have been speaking of a woman she had known well, a woman who had been her friend and whose mind and opinions she was familiar with.

I was astonished. 'To Winifred?' I said. 'A debt? What do you mean?' I had thought of my paper as the payment of my final dues to Winifred.

'You owe it to the beautiful thing you and Winifred had together for thirty years to at least *try* to look for the answers to your questions. Why you didn't write your book on massacre. Why you didn't ask your father what he really did during the war. There are service records. If we bother to look for these things, there is evidence of them to be found. You owe it to yourself and to Winifred to face up to the truth of all that. If you don't, you'll have failed to make sense of your life.'

I forgot I was driving and listened to her lecturing with astonishment.

'You owe it to your generation.' Now she turned in her seat and looked at me. 'You owe it to my generation. You said so yourself. You owe it to me. An apology is just a start. That's all it is. It's a start. It's not everything. That apology yesterday, it was beautiful. I haven't really thanked you properly for it. But it was just a start, Max.' She waited a moment. 'You're not offended, are you?'

'No,' I said, 'I'm not offended.'

'We're friends,' she said. 'Friends have to be able to be honest with each other, or what's the point of it?'

'Of course.'

'We all owe a debt to someone. My parents made an enormous sacrifice for me so I could go to university. I'm the only one in the whole family to have ever gone to university. If we don't pay our debts, we can't go on believing in ourselves. We're just empty. We're nothing. We're a joke.'

'Yes,' I said. 'You are right.'

'Our lives are meaningless if we give in,' she said. 'We can't just give in, Max. We have to fight. Or *they've* won and we've lost.'

I realised that she was talking about herself.

'Why you didn't insist on knowing the truth about your father is the biggest thing in your life. It's affected your whole life. It haunts you, but you don't do anything about it.' She looked across at me as if she expected me to argue with her. 'How *unreal* is that? You like to pretend you're too old and that it's all finished for you. But that's your game. That's the way you excuse yourself from having to do anything. You just have to have the guts to break your stupid vow of silence and ask your questions before it really is too late.' She sat up straighter. 'Shouldn't we be in that lane over there?'

I swerved across the two lanes and just made it into the airport turnoff.

She looked at me and laughed. 'You're a bloody rotten driver, Max.'

'Sorry,' I said.

She began to hum a tune.

'What is that?' I asked her after a minute or two.

'Dad always sings it when Mum gets into a bad mood. I didn't realise I was humming it.'

Miraculously, without knowing how I had done it, I had found the correct entrance to the airport car park—if you know the Hamburg airport car park you will understand my feeling of triumph. I pulled into a vacant spot and parked. I turned to her. 'Here we are,' I said, as if I expected her to congratulate me. She said nothing. We got out of the car and I took her two enormous suitcases from the boot and set them on the concrete.

'You weren't even listening to me, were you?' she accused me.

'Of course I was,' I said. 'It was interesting. Who are you flying with?'

'You owe me, Max.' She glared at me in mock anger, then she tucked her arm into mine and pressed it to her side, just as she had the previous afternoon outside Warburg Haus. 'I'm organising a cultural studies conference at Sydney University in March,' she said. 'It's the first time I've been responsible for an international conference. There are a lot of people waiting to see me fall in a heap over this so they can say I told you so to the idiots who appointed me to this chair. It's my first semester in the job.' She looked at me steadily. 'You must come to my conference. I need you. Having a real live German professor of history on my side will silence the doubters. None of them will have the guts to stand up to you. They'll be all over you.'

I was hoping she was not going to let go of my arm just yet. 'But I am no longer a professor,' I protested. 'I am retired.'

'Don't try to wheedle your way out of it!' She looked at me seriously. 'We got drunk together. That means a lot where I come from. We told each other a few truths. You told me something you said you'd never told anyone before. I cherish that. You trusted me, Max. It's important to me. It feels good to be trusted. Now you have to pay your debt honourably.'

I felt faintly excited. Was it really possible? She had a way of making things seem possible that had ceased to seem possible.

'After an apology, reparations are due,' she said. 'You know that. You know your own history.'

'Reparations,' I said, echoing her.

'Yes, reparations. You know what I mean. After the conference, I'll take you up to North Queensland to meet Uncle Dougald. He'll show you his country. Uncle Dougald's country is full of beautiful secrets you guys have never dreamed of. You can give a paper in Sydney on why you didn't ask your father what he did in the war. You'll have a few months to think about it. It will be a start. When you get back to the apartment today you can begin.' She shook me gently. 'Stop pretending you're a lost cause. It's not interesting.' She leaned and kissed me on the cheek, then she drew away and smiled her soft, vulnerable smile and pushed herself from my side, as if she were pushing off in a boat. 'We've got time for a coffee.'

We each dragged one of her wheeled suitcases through the car park and into the reception hall of the airport. She stood looking for her check-in counter. 'Just for that minute yesterday,' she said, 'when you turned away and left us all standing there by the door of Warburg Haus—you know?—you silenced us. We didn't know what to think. We were each waiting for someone else to be the first to say something. You changed what we were thinking. You cut across our assumptions about ourselves.

About the whole thing. It was impressive. It was a good moment. It was something I don't want to forget. The way you came up to us and apologised. It was beautiful. You know what I mean? We could see you didn't know how good it was and that it had sort of taken you by surprise too. We all thought at first that you were coming up to defend yourself in the usual way. You caught us off guard. After something like that you can't just go back to being silent, can you? Silence is no longer an option for you after something like that, is it? Silence would make a mockery of it all. We have to take the next step.'

We?

She checked her luggage and got a boarding pass and we took the escalator to the cafeteria. She pulled out a chair and sat in it. 'Get me a double-strength espresso.' She reached and took hold of my arm. 'And, hey!'

I waited.

'I speak my mind, Max. I don't keep silent. We've got more than enough of that deep silence stuff over there too.' She waved me away. 'Get me a coffee.'

I bought two coffees and carried them back to our table. When I sat down she said, 'You should see yourself. Did you look in a mirror this morning? You look like crap.' She laughed. 'Winifred wouldn't want to know you. Hey! Cheer up! We'll be seeing each other in Sydney in March.'

I stirred sugar into my coffee. 'I would like to come,' I said. I looked up and met her eyes. 'I'm not sure I can.'

'You don't have a choice. It's either come to my conference, or it's go back to the apartment and do what you were thinking of doing yesterday.' She sipped at the hot coffee and closed her eyes. 'You decide.'

I watched her. 'You saved my life,' I said.

'Bullshit!'

'It's not bullshit,' I said. 'It's the truth.' Suddenly I could not bear the thought of knowing I was never going to see her again. 'I'll come to your conference,' I said.

She looked at me, as surprised as I was to hear it. 'Is that a promise?'

'I guess.'

She leaned and kissed me on the cheek. 'That was easy.'

'I want to come.'

'I knew you would!' she said happily. 'I ought to call you Mad Max.' She took my hand in hers and examined it, counting my fingers as if she might be about to recite the nursery rhyme, *This little piggy went to market*. 'For a guy who's spent his entire life reading books, how come you've got such nice strong hands?'

'I was a farm labourer once, with my uncle, during the war.'

She relinquished my hand. 'Go to London and see your daughter and your grandchildren for Christmas.'

'You like to give advice,' I said.

'Some people need advice.'

I walked with her to the security barrier. Before she went through she embraced me, holding me strongly against her ample body. With her mouth close to my ear she whispered, 'Take care, Uncle Max!' She released me and turned and walked through the barrier. On the other side, she looked back and waved and blew me a kiss.

I waved and stood watching until she was out of sight. Professor Vita McLelland, the black princess of the barbarous new order. I missed her the moment she was gone. I turned away and went in search of the Peugeot. I had no idea where in the vast car park I had left it. It didn't seem to matter greatly. If I couldn't find it, I would take a taxi home and save myself the anxiety of the drive. I stood looking along the endless ranks of parked cars thinking about her. She had insisted that we were friends and that our friendship mattered to her. I was grateful to her and was shamed by my timidity, by the fragility of my morale. I realised I no longer felt alone. The image of the old man crossing the road in the rain suddenly rose up before me, and I silently apologised to him for having hated him for that moment. I saw then that I was standing next to the Peugeot.

Mount Nebo

5

A sense of arrival

Mount Nebo was the name of the remote township in the ranges of the Central Highlands of Queensland where Vita's uncle, Dougald Gnapun, lived. Despite its name, I could see no mountain from the summit of which I might expect to catch a glimpse of the Promised Land before I died. Indeed the silence of the township, and the low grey scrub surrounding it, was so unnatural that I felt as if I had arrived at the moment of stillness after the end of the world.

Vita and I had seen no one when we drove into town along the forlorn main street. It was late in the afternoon and the shops were empty, the buildings apparently abandoned, their yards and sideways neglected and overgrown with weeds and small bushes. There was not a vehicle nor a pedestrian to be seen. The only sign of life was a Shell service station at a crossroads, and even this had the appearance of being temporarily unattended.

A kilometre or two back along the road in from the coast Vita had pointed out the towers and gantries of a coal mine. 'That's what killed the town,' she told me. 'They built their own residential compound and stores. It's all air-conditioned. So who needs the town?'

As I stood there beside Dougald and his three dogs at the side gate of his house watching Vita drive into the distance in her bright little hire car, I realised that it must be the throbbing of the machinery of the mine that I could hear. It was a sound that emphasised the uncanny stillness within which we were encompassed. Then a rooster crowed nearby. It was as if a signal had been given to begin, but nothing stirred.

When Vita's car was lost to our sight over a distant rise, Dougald continued to stand looking down the road. Did he expect her to return and to announce that she had forgotten something or that she had changed her mind and had decided to stay with us? The dogs knew better, however, and lost interest in the vigil. Standing there in the perfect stillness beside Dougald, the fine red dust of Vita's departure drifting between us and the sinking sun, the expectant silence of the landscape seemed to open around me and I experienced a sense of anticipation. I looked at Dougald. He smiled, as if he took my meaning. Then he picked up my suitcase and carried it into the house.

I followed him. He was not the fierce square-jawed axe-wielding Scot that I had imagined, but a gentle, large-bodied man of my own age, a widower for considerably longer than I, soft looking and considered in his movements. He was darker than Vita, a good head taller than me, and, as I was soon to discover, inhabited a deep and very private silence of his own—as some poet has expressed it, *listening to his own depth*. His small, square, unpainted fibro-cement house was set on an irregular fenced block of land in alignment with the dusty gravel road on the extreme edge of the town, isolated from other dwellings. The house was not more than two hundred metres from the river and the commencement of the low grey scrub that extended to the horizon in all directions beyond the town's perimeters, except to the south, where softly rounded hills, or small mountains—among them, perhaps, the Mount Nebo of the town's name—broke the monotony of the level horizon line. I did not know then that these modest hills could only be seen for a short time after sunrise each morning and in the evening, when the atmosphere was clear of the ochreous haze that otherwise obscured any distant prospect during the heat of the day.

The room to which Dougald showed me was a small cell with a narrow uncurtained window which looked onto the empty road. A single bed stood against the wall beside the window. Next to the bed there was an upended wooden crate of the kind that had been in service when I was a boy and which might once have contained a dozen bottles, of beer perhaps or soft drink. It was the only object in the room with which I felt the faintest kinship of familiarity. Opposite the door there was a varnished cupboard, its single door hanging open. Dougald set down my suitcase beside the bed and went over to the cupboard and closed its door. He turned and looked at me. Behind him the door of the wardrobe silently swung open again.

'If there's anything you need, old mate,' he said, his voice soft and encouraging. He might have been welcoming me back to this room after a period of absence. He took out his mobile telephone and frowned at it, perhaps reading a message, or considering sending one.

I thanked him and said the room would do fine and that I would let him know if I needed anything. 'Where is the bathroom?' I asked.

He led me back through the kitchen and out onto the square of concrete behind the house. He indicated an enclosed water-tank stand. 'The shower's in there. She's not too bad this time of year.' He turned and pointed towards the back of the yard. A path through the grass led to a wire enclosure in which a dozen or so brown hens and a rooster were penned. Beside the hen run there was a narrow shed constructed of timber slabs with a door at the front. The door of this modest building, like the door of the wardrobe, hung open. 'That's the toilet,' he said. Behind the toilet, beyond the back fence, was an open field in which three large yellow bulldozers, rusting and overgrown with creepers, had evidently been abandoned. 'See them tall trees? The river's down there,' he said, pointing. 'She's not much just now. We haven't had any decent rains this year.' He examined the screen of his telephone again. He seemed to be expecting a call.

Alone in the small bare room that was to be mine for the duration of my visit, I stood at the window and looked along the deserted road. I had not felt so abandoned to strangeness since the day my mother left me at my uncle's farm when I was a boy. If Vita had still been with us, I would have carried my suitcase out to her car and sat in the passenger seat with my arms folded and insisted she drive me back to civilisation. *I have nothing against your uncle. Indeed, he seems to be a most sympathetic man. But why, Vita, why have you brought me to this place?* The peculiar feeling of anticipation that I had experienced for a moment while standing outside with Dougald was gone. I listened for the sound of the mine machinery, but I could not make it out from inside the house. I suddenly realised I was exhausted. We had travelled for hours in the car over rough roads after leaving the airport at the coastal town and my back was aching, the pain going down into my left hip. I examined the bed linen. The sheets were freshly laundered and the blanket smelled pleasantly of wool. I realised it was new. The pillow, too, was generous and soft, its white case still creased from its first unfolding. The smell of the bed was of fresh linen and home. I had not expected it, and felt a flood of gratitude towards Dougald for this consideration. I took off my shoes and lay on the bed, my arms by my sides. My left leg throbbed steadily from the referred pain in my spine. I gave a small groan and closed my eyes. *My dearest, you do not know where I am.*

* * *

A ground mist hovered like a softly levitating bed sheet above the open field beyond the hen run, the abandoned bulldozers a looming family of dreaming pachyderms. All was silent, except for the distant throbbing of the mine. Dougald and I were at the back fence. He had fed the hens and I had collected seven warm brown eggs from their boxes.

'We'd better shift her peg,' he said. His voice caressed the words, as if he spoke in order to listen to himself, in order to hear a human voice in this place. Lifting his hand, he pointed at the freckle-faced nanny-goat. She had cropped almost to the earth the growth of weeds and grasses within the compass of her tether.

Dougald's pace was unhurried and the sun was well up and the day already warm by the time we returned to the house. While he cooked breakfast, I sat at the kitchen table leafing through a collection of old newspapers and magazines. He had set his mobile phone down among a confusion of documents and a laptop computer which occupied the end of the table nearest the door. I wondered what business it was that occupied him here in this out-of-the-way place on the edge of the wilderness. He set down a plate of eggs, bacon and toast on the table in front of me, then brought his own and sat down. We were seated side by side facing the open door, as if we were twins or old brothers, the view of the patch of concrete and the antique gum tree before us, the sunlit yard and outbuildings beyond, the goat grazing her new range contentedly.

We ate our breakfast in silence, as if we were about to embark upon some hazardous enterprise. During breakfast Dougald received two calls on his mobile telephone. He rose from the table each time with a soft apology and took the phone and stood with it at the back door, murmuring into it in such a low voice he might have been conversing with the dead. He said nothing to me of these calls but set the telephone aside when he was done and resumed his breakfast. I was sensitive of my status as a newly arrived guest in his house and did not feel at liberty to question him about his situation. I was curious, nevertheless, to know why he had remained in this town, since it had been abandoned by most of its other inhabitants. Had he stayed on from an attachment to his ancestral country?

From his self-enclosed manner I took it that he had no particular wish to speak about himself. He seemed content with the silence between us. It was not in the least an awkward silence. In fact I do not recall ever being so at ease with a new acquaintance in such a close domestic situation as I was in those early days with Dougald. His silence was a contrast to Vita's unceasing flow of conversation, which I had found tiring after a few days with her in Sydney. Everything Vita felt, she felt intensely. There were no half-measures with her. At the end of each day with her at the conference I had retired to my hotel room with a headache. She had promised to return to Mount Nebo for me in a week or two, and had repeated her assurance that her uncle would take me to see his country.

His dog, a pale-eyed wolf-like bitch, waited in attendance at the side of his chair, and every so often he offered her a morsel of bacon, which she nipped delicately from between his fingers with her bared front teeth, her ears laid back along her narrow skull. She did not beg or demand these favours, but was fastidious and correct, waiting patiently, her tail sweeping from side to side, her gaze steady on his right hand. She was satisfied with her master's generosity and confident it would not arbitrarily be withdrawn. The two brown dogs, her offspring and members of her tribe, made no attempt to enter the house, but stood in the open doorway looking in enviously at their privileged mother, lifting their snouts and sniffing the air. When I finished my breakfast I went over to them and gave them the fat from my bacon, which they greatly appreciated.

I took my own and Dougald's plates to the sink and set about washing the accumulation of dirty dishes and pans that had obviously been piled there for some time. There were old scraps of food and half-eaten pieces of mouldy toast among the dishes. While I did the washing-up, Dougald made several phone calls. As he talked he walked back and forth across the small space of the kitchen, from the cupboards to the open doorway then back again, looking down at his feet all the while, and might have been a prisoner measuring the confines of his cell. He was observed closely all the while by his grey bitch. She stood forward on her trembling forelegs, eager for a sign from him, her pale eyes never leaving his face. The two brown dogs lost interest in the goings-on in the kitchen once they saw there was no more food to be had. They sat at their ease out in the yard in the shade of the great broken gum tree, their forepaws crossed, their attention on the goat, which had managed to force its head through the wire fence and was attempting to reach a tall blue thistle growing just beyond the range of its tether rope. The larger of the two dogs gave a low woof every now and then and glanced towards the kitchen, wishing to reassure us that it was not just idling but was on duty. Dougald had not named his dogs and asked nothing of them, not issuing them with either commands or reprimands.

The day was warm and still outside, and in the kitchen there was the domestic clatter of the dishes as I set them aside on the draining board, behind me the low murmur of Dougald's voice as he spoke into his telephone. The plain white dishes in my hands and the feel of the warm suds on my fingers insisted upon an intimate acknowledgment of homeliness and familiarity. Scrubbing at the remains of burned food that clung to the insides of the pots, I found it difficult to recall with any certainty the conditions of my former life. I turned from the sink and looked towards Dougald. He caught my look and smiled. It was a slow, gracious, kindly, amused smile that drew up the loose folds of his cheeks and formed deep recesses and wrinkles around his eyes. There was much in his smile of understanding, and much was communicated to me of a sensitive response in him to our situation together in his home. I returned his smile. It was surely our amusement that we acknowledged, this vision of ourselves as two old men together at the end of their days. We might indeed have been brothers who had never married but had remained in the modest family home long after the deaths of our parents, I assuming the role of housekeeper, and he that of breadwinner.

I turned back to the sink and went on scrubbing contentedly at the frying pan. I was thinking about an incident far in my past. It must have been 1943 when I met her, a few months before the destruction of Hamburg by Allied bombing. I was a child, but in my daydreams then I thought myself a man—that ideal condition to which all boys aspire. My father was away at the front, and with the growing threat of bombing my mother had taken me out of Hamburg to stay with her older brother on his farm. I do not know why my mother did not take my sister to the farm also, but can only suppose she did not think it suitable for a girl to be left alone there. One evening, when I was returning to the farmhouse through the hazel coppice from the ploughed field where my uncle was working, a gipsy girl stepped into my path from the concealment of the hazels. She laughed to see my fear, her bright headscarf lifting in the evening breeze. I knew myself to be at once in her power. In that moment, charged with fear and intuition, she might have appeared before me to deliver a prophecy of my death. Or perhaps, if she were to find me worthy of it, to present me with a gift that would empower me to alter the course of my history. But she only asked me for bread. *Give me bread!* she demanded. But I had no bread and was not yet man enough to invite her to accompany me to the farmhouse, where I might have found bread and sausage for her in the larder. So instead of going to her aid, I stood dumbfounded by her beauty and by the strange power over me which she seemed to possess, my gaze fixed on her, my hands clasped behind my back.

Her family had been murdered, she told me, and she laughed a strange unnerving laugh as she told it. It was as if she spoke of people she had known long ago, almost in another life, and whose reality she had already begun to forget. Their brutal slaughter, she said, and there was a calm in her eyes and in her voice as she said it that terrified me, their brutal slaughter had taken place before her in the early hours of that very morning. She was alone and on the run. That is how I have remembered her, as if she knew no other existence than to be alone and on the run. When she laughed it seemed to me then, just as it seems to me now, that it was not she but I who was the lost one. Although she can have been little older than I was, within the glowing shadows of the hazel coppice that evening she seemed to me ageless and wise and deeper in her experience of life than I could ever hope to be, and I felt that nothing of my inner life, my past or my future, was hidden from her, but was hidden only from myself. Indeed I knew it to be so, with that deep intuition of knowing that is the private truth of such things for each of us, and which we cannot share with another without forfeiting its mysterious power to compel our imagination.

Standing at the sink in Dougald's kitchen that morning, my hands in the warm washing-up water, my heart contracted at the remembrance of the gipsy girl. Had she escaped? Or had she been caught and suffered a hideous death? I still longed to know, all those years later, that she had made her escape. I still longed to be reassured that her meeting with me that evening had been for her a saving moment in her hazardous journey alone through the hostile world. More than half a century after my meeting with her, I wanted to believe that she had lived and had known happiness and contentment in life. I still regretted not giving her bread and shelter that evening. I still regretted not offering her the means to live while the precious opportunity to do so had been mine. The passage of years and decades is nothing to such memories. One lifetime is not long enough to forget these things. For me the gipsy girl still smiled her enigmatic smile, knowing something she did not disclose to me that evening in the hazel coppice of our childhood. Guilt, I discovered that evening, was not the experience only of the heartless perpetrator of a crime, but was a complex and pervasive condition of the human soul, as intractable and as mysterious as love.

When I finished drying the dishes and found places for them on the shelves of the cupboard, we drove into the town in Dougald's old red pick-up truck to collect the stores and mail. The only store in the town was at the Shell service station. It was also the only bank and served as the post office. Three times a week, unless there had been heavy rains and the road had been washed out, stores and medicines and other necessities of life were brought by the carrier from the coast. This enterprise was cheerfully conducted by a handsome woman in her early fifties. She was the wife of a miner who had been injured some years before in an accident at the coal mine and since then had been confined to a wheelchair. She and her crippled husband purchased the business with his compensation payout. I observed that Dougald and she exchanged a certain light and agreeable banter with each other which was suggestive of the enjoyment of a deeper intimacy than either of them was prepared to acknowledge openly in my presence. When we were driving home Dougald cleared his throat and said, as if he felt the need to offer me an explanation, 'Whenever I have to go down to the coast for a few days on business, Esmé looks after the place for me.'

I said, 'She seems to be a very capable woman.'

I saw his house from the road as we approached it, and recognised the small square uncurtained window of my own room. He turned into the driveway and the two brown dogs ran out to meet us.

6

What men gather

Dougald seemed to me to be waiting for something, and for now he asked no more of me than he asked of his dogs. One fine still day followed another with little to distinguish them, and it seemed no time at all before two weeks of this measured existence had gone by. I had no desire to bring to an end just yet this peculiar sojourn with Dougald in his little house on the edge of the abandoned township. One day I would be required to go back to my life and to take up once again the problem of how to live it, but for now there was nothing to be done. I was determined to enjoy this leave of absence from the responsibility to live with purpose.

It was a little after noon and I was standing outside the kitchen on the patch of concrete in the shade of the gum tree. I had been refreshing the water for the hens and the goat and still carried the blue plastic bucket in the crook of my right arm. I enjoyed being out in the open air and found a certain modest satisfaction in the performance of these daily chores. I was aware that my small service left Dougald free to attend to his paperwork and the numerous telephone calls he received throughout each day. Before going in to prepare our lunch, I had paused on the concrete patch outside the kitchen to enjoy the calm beauty of the day. The two brown dogs lay spreadeagled and panting at my feet, waiting to discover what I was to do next, when Dougald came out of the kitchen and handed me his mobile telephone. 'It's Vita, old mate,' he said, and went back inside the kitchen.

She apologised for not calling sooner. 'It's been frantic here,' she said. Then, without pausing, she asked briskly, 'So, Max, tell me, how are you and Dougald getting on?' It was as if she referred to a business arrangement and was expecting a report from me on my progress with our project of *getting on* with her Uncle Dougald.

I said, 'We are getting on very well. In fact we are an old domestic couple. I do the chores and leave him free to do his work.' I waited to hear what she would say to this, but she said nothing. 'Should I say more?'

'Don't let him work too hard,' she said. 'If you let him, he'll just work and do nothing else.'

What did she expect of me? 'In the evening after dinner,' I said, 'once he has abandoned his work for the day and I have washed the dishes and made us a final cup of tea, we drowse in front of the television for an hour. Eventually we bestir ourselves and say goodnight and we go to our separate rooms. Really there is very little else to report.'

'You sound happy?' she said almost resentfully, and might have been accusing me of a moral lapse.

'Should I not be then?' I asked her.

'Happily *married*, by the sound of it,' she said and laughed cheerlessly. 'How is he?'

'Dougald seems to me to be in fine spirits.'

'He's not a well man, Max,' she corrected me. 'We've been worried about him ever since Aunty May died. It's nearly five years now and he hasn't moved on.'

Did she think, I wondered, that *I* had moved on? I considered mentioning to her Dougald's delicate friendship with Esmé at the service station. I thought of offering this to her as evidence that he had indeed moved on a considerable way from the state of paralysed anguish into which he must have been cast by the death of his wife. But I felt it would have been a betrayal to speak of this to her, and so I said nothing. Had Vita been a man, I would have seen no betrayal in telling her about Esmé. How we are forever adjusting the truth.

'He hasn't taken a break since he lost Aunty May,' she said. 'In a perverse sort of way I think he almost wants to make himself ill.'

'I can understand that,' I said.

'You've seen him, he just slaves away for his people day and night. They *use* him. He doesn't know how to say no. It's sad, Max. It's wearing him down.'

Dougald had not spoken to me about his work, but I had gathered a general impression of what it was he did. 'He seems to be saddled with a great number of reports and submissions,' I said. 'His situation reminds me a little of my old situation with the bureaucracy at the university. But he seems very capable of getting on with it.'

'They sit on their arses and let him do everything for them,' she said. 'They never think of saying thank you or offering to help him. The minute he settles one issue for them they're after him for something else. How many times a day does that phone of his ring? It's his own fault. He hasn't trained anyone up to replace him. He thinks he's the only one who can do anything. He treats them as if they're children. And like children they grumble and do nothing.' She was silent a moment, then she said, 'See if you can talk him into taking you out for a trip for a few days. Get him to show you a bit of his country. Get him away from that phone. Tell him you want to see something of the place before you go home. It will do him good to get out into the bush. It's what he needs. He loves being out in the bush. He's a changed man out there. Do you think you can do that for me, Max?'

I said I would do my best, but that I did not consider it to be my place as his guest to offer Dougald advice on how he should conduct himself. She was contemptuous of my reply and accused me of being stuffy and European. 'For God's sake, Max, just bloody do it, can't you?' she said. 'It's not asking the impossible, is it? You two guys understand each other. You're both in the same boat. You both lost your wives.'

I stood there for a moment considering what she had said. 'You planned this,' I said.

'You're happy aren't you? You just said you were happy. What's the problem?'

'You're obviously not going to be satisfied with me just doing the household chores for him.'

'Are *you*?'

'This is not the situation you gave me to understand it to be,' I said. I could hear myself beginning to sound pompous—the old man she had hoped to silence. I was disappointed. I didn't want to be responsible for Dougald. I could hear voices in the background and the sound of doors closing.

'Sorry,' she said. 'Someone came in. What were you saying?'

'If Dougald is going to show me this Promised Land of his,' I said, 'then I shall have to earn the right to see it. Is that it? You had this in mind as early as Hamburg, didn't you?' I hoped I was not sounding too severe.

'It was for you too,' she said. She sounded tired, suddenly, and as if she were losing interest. 'I wasn't using you. I just thought it would be nice for both of you if you were to meet. I thought you would get on. But maybe I was wrong.'

'We do get on,' I said. 'You were right. We get on very well.'

'It was for you too.'

I said, 'You sound tired.'

'I *am* tired.'

'Why don't you come up and spend some time with us?'

'This place will fall apart if I leave it.'

'I haven't felt as relaxed in years,' I said.

'So there, you *are* happy. You're glad I took you up there, aren't you?'

'I am more than glad, Vita. I am grateful. But you should take a holiday yourself.'

'I will as soon as I get through this next bit.' Her tone softened. 'I'm sorry if I sounded like a bitch just now. You take care, Uncle Max. I love you both, you know. I have to go now, they're screaming for me in the meeting.'

I went into the kitchen and set the phone on the table beside Dougald. He did not look up or say anything. He was typing, very rapidly, on the keyboard of his laptop, his papers spread around him. His wire-framed spectacles clung to the very tip of his large nose like a stick insect clinging to a knobbly old tree branch. It did not seem to be the right moment to urge him to leave his work and go gallivanting off into the scrub with me. I was not sure I wanted to go into the scrub, anyway. It looked boundless, like the sea, vast and grey and inhospitable, and not a place where human beings were meant to spend their days. Even with Dougald as my guide, I found the thought of venturing into it intimidating. I was content to stay with our present arrangements until it was time for me to leave.

As I turned away he looked up and gestured with his hand, turning towards the open door, where the two brown dogs stood looking in at us. 'These two fellers were glad to see you get here, Max.' He looked at me and grinned, his features almost boyish in the soft reflected light from the open doorway.

I looked at the dogs with him. 'Yes. We are good friends,' I said. I understood him to be proposing, with his gently indirect sense of the comic, that the true purpose of my visit was to serve the contentment of these two dogs. I wondered how much of my conversation with Vita he had overheard. His own wolf-like bitch was his jealous and constant companion, but before I arrived the brown dogs must have known themselves to be without a master, surely the unhappiest condition for a dog. They had taken to sleeping under the house beneath my bedroom at night, from where I heard them snuffling and whimpering in their dreams. They were ready, I dare say, to shake the dust from their coats at a moment's notice and accompany me should I decide to get up and venture out into the night. At which, unlike a human companion, they would not tax me with the question, *Where are we going at this late hour?*, but would trot beside me, or scout ahead, knowing their purpose satisfied in being my companions. At Dougald's remark they knew themselves spoken of and they lifted their muzzles and snapped at each other playfully.

Dougald said, 'I'm going down to Mackay for a couple of days. If there's anything you need while I'm away, Esmé will take care of it for you.' He looked at me steadily.

I thanked him, then I went over to the refrigerator and began to prepare our lunch.

My bedroom was whitely illuminated, as if a comet were passing across the sky. Then it plunged abruptly into darkness again. I sat up, listening. I could hear—or perhaps I felt it—the faint tremor of the mine. There was no knock or call. The house was silent, the dogs sounding no alarm. A car door slammed, followed at once by the sound of a vehicle driving away, its tyres crunching on the gravel of the sideway. I wondered if I should get up and investigate, but decided not to.

I must have slept again, for when I woke the light of morning filled my room. I got up and put on my dressing-gown and went out into the kitchen. There was no sign of Dougald. I knew he had gone, but even so I pushed the door of his bedroom open and spoke his name. I had never been into his room. It was as plain as my own. A double bed with varnished timber ends was pushed against the far wall, the bedding roughly tossed aside. A tumbler and a small old-fashioned transistor radio stood on a cabinet next to the bed. He must have played the radio very softly, as I had never heard it. Scattered about on the floor were several open packets. I recognised them at once as packaging from those life-saving drugs without which our kind soon cease to endure. His sulking bitch was sprawled on a piece of sacking at the bed end, one grey eye fixed on me malevolently. She drew back her lips in a snarl and raised her head. I withdrew and went into the kitchen and set the electric jug to boil.

It was a strange feeling to be alone there, knowing Vita's expectations. Things had changed. I was not sure yet whether I liked the change. While I waited for the water to boil for my tea I stood in the open doorway looking out into the sunlit yard. The brown dogs came from under the house and stood with me, scratching and yawning and considering the prospects of the day. I said, 'Well, boys, we are on our own.' The goat was watching me from the far side of the yard, her head up and her ears pricked, alert for a sign from me. I signalled to her with a wave of my hand, wishing to reassure her that I would soon be over there attending to her needs. I would do my duty, there was no doubt about that, whether I wanted to or not. I decided to give her a treat of the sweet grainy mash that Dougald kept for the hens. It seemed unfair to me that she should be the only one among us to live out her days tethered.

I set off along the path with the bucket of mash after breakfast, closely attended by my two brown dogs. A sudden unaccountable rush of optimism took hold of me at that moment, and I stood looking around at the scene, astonished by the perfect isolation, the absolute stillness of this strangely pointless place. The morning was bright and cool, the air sweet and pungent with some flowering herb, the vast unbroken sweep of the scrubs to the south, where they met the soft rounding of the distant hills, visible at this time of day, behind me the small grey house and the outbuildings overlooked by the great broken tree. There was a familiarity in it all that moved me suddenly. I looked into the sky and saw a flight of birds sweep across the blue above me, their cries like the cries of excited children at play. I would soon be gone from here and would never return, and all this would be a memory. Could I counterfeit Dougald's existence here? Be him in his absence? Alone and attending to the routine of my days, suspecting nothing of the existence of the old German professor, Max Otto? But of course I knew I could not counterfeit with assurance his deep attachment to this place. His attachment to his *country*, as Vita spoke of it, employing the word as if she spoke not of the nation to which he belonged, nor of a love of country, but as if she touched upon an ancestral knowing grappled into the roots of his being so deeply that even he knew its influence only as an uncanny intuition—as if his country required something from him, a sacrifice, perhaps, or a homage of some kind, but not something he could name or on which he could place his hand and say, *Here it is.* Did his country make a call on him and on his capacities which he felt as an anchoring to this place? Was it a bond, indeed a bondage, that went beyond mere familiarity and a knowledge of things? If his country was his calling, then I could not counterfeit that.

The goat ate her bowl of mash daintily, making small bleating sounds of pleasure, and pausing to look up at me every few seconds, an expression of curiosity in her intelligent eyes. I saw what a truly beautiful animal she was. With what astonishment the whole world must have prized her had she been the only one of her kind, instead of one of the commonest of creatures. Looking into the velvety depths of her eyes I could not believe that she did not enjoy a reflective inner life. When I attempted to stroke her neck she drew back sharply and stood off from me, stamping her hoof, as if she rebuked me for this uncalled-for liberty, eyeing me angrily. Despite the indignity of her tether she was clearly a creature of great refinement.

When she had fastidiously cleaned the last of the mash from the sides of the bowl, I returned with it and the bucket to the shed where Dougald stored the bags of feed, which he kept by the door in two aluminium drums with fitted lids to keep the vermin out. The shed was solidly constructed of heavy slabs of split timber and was a much earlier building than the house. The timbers still bore the marks of the adze with which they had been expertly squared to fit snugly one against the other. A red brick chimney stood at the end furthest from the door, and a small square window was set in one of the side walls. It was really more a one-roomed cottage than a shed. I supposed it to have been the original dwelling, where Dougald and his family had lived when he was a boy. It stood on the far side of the gum tree, beside the lean-to in which Dougald kept his truck. The timber slabs had been patched with flattened tin where they had come apart or been eaten by insects. Over time these patches of tin had themselves rusted to the thinness of lace, the raised embossment of the sign of a shell still visible here and there—an enduring advertisement of their original contents.

I set the bucket and the bowl aside on the lid of one of the drums and stood by the door looking in at the dim interior. When I stepped into the gloom, it was with the same feeling of guilty trespass I had known as a boy whenever I nosed about my uncle's house while he was away working in the fields. The dim interior of the cottage was shot through with bright blades of sunlight, in which dust motes floated like worlds journeying in distant galaxies. The air was musty with the reek of damp earth and the droppings of vermin. It was the smell of the sheds and byres of my childhood. I took hold of the cool shank of an iron bar that leaned against the wall beside me and made to lift it. Its weight resisted me, however, and I set it back in its place. I felt rebuked by, and secretly ashamed of, the weakness of my old man's arm. Next to the bar was a collection of shovels and spades, their handles and blades of varying sizes and styles according to the uses for which they had been designed. On the dirt floor beside these was an assortment of worn axe heads, mauls, iron wedges and other tools. Most of the tools were from my uncle's period and I well understood their utility. They were history. Another age. My childhood and my youth. A lost time. They would have puzzled a young man from this age and he would have looked on them as antiques. There were other implements, arrangements of chains, levers and pulleys, the uses of which were unknown to me. By the careful manner with which these things had been set against the wall it was clear they had not been discarded but had been put aside with a habitual concern for the morrow. No doubt set there in their customary places at the end of a day's work, in the expectation that their owner would return and make use of them again in the morning—it is as well we do not know our last occasions.

I stepped over sacks and boxes, and ducked beneath bunches of steel-jawed rabbit traps that hung from the rafters by twisted lengths of wire, like the skeletons of roosting bats. My uncle had set such traps at the boundaries of his fields, where the open country met the woodland and the rabbits came out at evening to feed on the tender shoots of his corn. When I reached up and touched them they clinked with a sound so familiar it made me catch my breath, and I saw my uncle crouched on the earth and in the action of reaching behind him to shake loose one of these demonic appliances from the bundle, his shoulders lifting as he pressed on the spring and set the plate. I could *smell* him, that man who had remained a mystery to me all my life, the peculiar acid sweat of him, as of a nervous animal. I had feared him, knowing him to be strange, a man obsessed with the fertility of his soil almost to the point of madness.

Odd pieces of harness, straps, buckles and horse blankets hung from the roof beams alongside the rabbit traps. The leather was grey and dry as biscuit to the touch. This suspension of forgotten things from the rafters among the weird shadows of the old cottage looked like racks of meat in an abandoned smokehouse. I made my way with care to the very back. In front of the fireplace, straddling a wooden trestle, were two saddles, the horsehair stuffing spilling from their pads where the rats had been gathering materials to line their nests. An iron cooking stove stood within the dark cavity of the fireplace. On one of the stove's hotplates was a pile of stretched rabbit skins. When I picked up the topmost skin the light shone through it and I saw that it had been eaten through by moths and worms. The prepared skins may have been readied for a buyer who had never come back to claim.

them. I turned to leave the cottage and struck my shin against something. I bent and lifted it out of the way. It was a child's tricycle. Had it been Dougald's? With care I put it to one side.

Outside, the dogs greeted me and I stood and breathed the sweet fresh air. So much is forgotten. So much remembered. The trivial and the minute sit before us as if we experienced them only yesterday, and the greatest events are forgotten. Did I remember the day the war began? No, I did not. But I did remember the first day my sister attended school, an event that took place in the same year—and I remembered my uncle's smell! The smell of human anxiety, rancid and sharp. There is much memory in a smell.

7

Seven eggs

Perhaps I had shouted or gesticulated. I had been dreaming of my uncle's farm and woke knowing the occasion of the dream. Its narrative was intricate, extensive, cluttered and unclear, but it was, I knew at once, associated with Dougald's old cottage. I felt as if the dream had been going on all night. I reached to the end of the bed for my dressing-gown and draped it around my shoulders. Through my uncurtained window the moon was a half-disc in the star-filled sky: patient, placid, an eternal observer—I might have been marooned on a drifting spaceship. The dream clung to my mind. It was still going on. I got out of bed and put on the light and looked into the kitchen. The door to the yard was open as I had left it. The tracery of the tree's shadows cast blackly onto the luminous ground of the concrete the bright first state of an etching. I could feel Dougald's absence, an intensification of the peculiar silence, throbbing faintly with the engines of the mine—the engines of my spaceship, nudging me deeper into the dark, cold, interstellar spaces.

I closed my bedroom door carefully, so as not to disturb the night, as if I feared to be really present there. I picked up my journal from the floor beside my bed and got in under the blankets. As soon as I began to write, my thoughts flowed effortlessly onto the page and I had no need to reflect on what I wrote, but set it down as it came to me. It was a story that was written in my heart. I am no longer the dreaming boy I was then. But what has changed? Inside, I mean. Nothing real. Nothing real has changed inside. All that is real has endured. Hopes, lusts, desires, dreams. All such stupidities as these have endured, even if I do not have the occasion to speak of them. And fear too. That also. It is all still with me. The strangeness of it all. The strangeness has endured. Here is what I wrote in my journal that night.

That first morning on my uncle's farm, when the light in the east was a splinter of anxiety along the horizon, my uncle woke me roughly from my sleep, shaking my shoulders and urging me, as if the house was on fire, 'Get up, Max! Get up!' I woke with fright, my heart hammering. We did not stop to eat breakfast, but when I was dressed he made me go with him at once, gripping me by my wrist, as if he arrested me, and striding a half-step ahead of me, his right leg describing a stiff arc before he planted it at each step, his shoulders dipping and rising with the laboured action of a man who hauls on a rope. Without a word more he led me in this manner to the distant field where he had been ploughing the previous day. There he grasped the collar of my coat and made me squat beside him in the headland furrow—was it his intention to bury me there, a living sacrifice to the fierce god of his soil? In the chill dawn light the earth glistened before my terrified gaze like freshly butchered meat, the sour-sweet smell of its breath in my nostrils.

My uncle took a handful of earth and held it up until it touched my face and I flinched. His pale blue eyes, in which there was something a little mad and

something of the wolf, searched mine, holding me
with his belief. He spoke to me in a voice that touched
an emotion in me I had not known existed until
that moment. It was neither quite the fascination of
desire, nor yet quite revulsion either, that I felt, but
a disquieting blend of the two; an emotion having its
obscure origins in that equivocal region of the human
psyche which urges us to gaze upon those things from
which we know we should, in all human decency, turn
our eyes away. 'This is our soil,' he said—as if he said,
this is your soul. 'We must care for it as we care for
our lives.' Even as a boy, at this first initiation, I knew
he spoke of something sacred to him, an indissoluble
aspect of his innermost sense of who he was; that
source from whence he had his origins. 'It is the soil
of our fathers,' he said, gazing wildly into my eyes, as
if he might begin to strike me about the head in his
passion, searching all the while with a hopeless kind
of desperation for evidence of my worthiness to share
his certainty. 'This soil is us!' he shouted, and he shook
me. 'We are this soil!' I would readily have agreed with
him, and would have shouted my belief back to him,
but I was too terrified and could not utter a sound.
What had I to do to please him? He snatched my

hand and thrust it into the newly turned furrow. 'This is who you are, Max!' He whispered to me fiercely, his face contorted and close to mine, his words catching in his throat. He might have been imparting to me the core of a mystical knowing that only my assent could confirm for him, as if something in him must doubt it until he saw it in another. I drew back, no doubt whimpering in terror, scarcely registering what he was saying, but expecting at any moment that he would jump on me in a wild, howling rage and stamp me into his earth. Suddenly, and with a sigh of resignation or weariness, and a flinging of his hands, he stood and lurched away along the furrow, leaving me crouching there. It was as if his madness exhausted him and he flung it from him like a garment that was preventing him from breathing. Like all madmen, however, he was not all mad.

At the edge of the field he stopped and looked back and called, beckoning to me. He waited until I came up to him, then he put his arm around my shoulders and said in a calm voice, 'I have been up all night,' as if this explained or excused his behaviour. We walked home together thus, his heavy arm over my shoulders like a bag of something we had dug out between us from a grave. I took his manner to be a kind of apology all the same, the best he could do. I was soon to learn that he looked upon his rages as if they were the actions of another and not his true self. He could be gentle, kind and thoughtful when the mood took him. Remembering him now, I remember him as two men who were not alike and who feared each other, as if two rival brothers inhabited the same body.

He was my mother's elder brother and had lived a solitary existence on the farm since the death of his parents, his one passion the rich dark earth of his forefathers—I was about to write, his unearthly passion. And so it was. I soon learned that he worshipped the soil in a desperate, hopeless way, as some men worship a woman whose affections they despair of ever winning. He looked on his bondage to the soil with longing and with loathing, tormented by his solitary enslavement to it, and exulting in its power to hold him. He had not married and had no son of his own, and it was soon evident to me that he hoped to win me to his faith while my father was away at the war and my mother and sister were in Hamburg. I was to become a son of the soil of our fatherland.

Such was his mad dream for me. I was to be his continuation. I was to make sense of his life for him. This, no less, was what he wanted from me. After my mother left me in his care he must have stayed up all that first night, aware of me sleeping under his roof, meditating on the means by which he could win me over. And so that wild initiation in the field at dawn, grabbing me by the arm and dragging me from my bed at the first hint of daylight. I think he afterwards realised he had overdone it and feared he might have alienated my sympathies for good.

The strangeness of his solitary existence on the farm frightened and fascinated me in equal measure, but I eventually came to regard him with a guarded affection. There is only one thing for which I have not forgiven him, but aside from that I recall him now more with sympathy than with dislike, seeing him not as an evil man, but as the bewildered victim of his own solitary intensities. The improvement of the fertility of their soil, which they understood themselves to be holding in trust for the generations of their kind, was in those days the obsessive preoccupation of many small landholders. The question of how many bushels of grain they and their neighbours had managed to harvest to the acre, or how many fat bullocks they had turned off that year, was a source of fierce rivalry between them. It was a rivalry that was not always friendly and which sometimes resulted in passionate hatreds that endured between neighbouring families from one generation to the next. As with all forms of madness, my uncle's madness had its origins in what usually passes with us for sanity.

Despite his bizarre tutelage that year I came to no physical harm, and in my solitary wanderings about the countryside I learned to love the gentle rural landscape inhabited by my uncle. He had a wooden leg, and had been exempted from military service. He had lost his right foot when he was a boy and was working with his father in the fields. He had lifted a leaf of the spike harrows at the headland to free the clods of grass that had accumulated underneath it, when the horse was startled—it was said by the whisper of a gipsy—and bolted. My uncle's foot was caught under the harrows and he was dragged the length of the field. The accident might have killed him, but he survived thanks to the skill of a retired surgeon who lived in the village. His right leg was amputated below the knee. In a cupboard under the stairs in the farmhouse, my uncle kept a collection of wooden legs of different sizes that he had worn at the successive stages of growing up. He showed them to me one evening, the way people show us old photographs of themselves when they were young, wishing us to share with them something of their pride in who they have become. I asked him why, when he had outgrown these legs, he and his parents had kept them, for surely neither he nor they could have imagined a future use for them. The legs leaned against each other in the corner of the cupboard, as if they were a little band of runners who rested there in order to regain their strength before continuing the journey, and for a long moment my uncle said nothing, but reached and touched first this one, then another, no doubt remembering himself at the stages of his life they represented to him— there were memories in those legs too. At length he turned to me. 'They are my legs, Max,' he said simply, and he smiled, as if he answered my uncertainty. It was a private, inward smile, however, and referred I think to a reality he believed to lie beyond my childish comprehension. In a darker mood, later that same evening as we sat at our supper in his kitchen, he said

to me, 'Your father is not at the front, but is engaged
on secret work.' Despite my youth it was clear to me
that he wished to suggest that my father's role in the
war was not an honourable one. I was sickened by
the charge and did not believe him. He watched me
closely to see how I took it. I looked down at my plate
and busied myself with my food, hiding my dismay
from him. 'Yes!' he said firmly. Then he banged the
handle of his knife on the table, so that I jumped with
fright, and he shouted, 'Yes!' It was the less ordered
brother breaking through and threatening me with
insanity if I resisted his representation of the truth
about my father, his despised brother-in-law, a man
he considered unworthy of his sister. Such things are
never simply what they seem to be.

I brooded for that whole year on what my uncle
had said about my father. And although my uncle did
not refer to it again it was like a dark secret we shared
and dared not speak of, and it remained thereafter a
cause of tension and distrust between us. When my
mother eventually came to the farm to take me home,
I told her what my uncle had said about my father
and asked her what she supposed him to have meant
by it. I kept my own understanding to myself and did

not speak openly of my fears to her. I remember the pained and weary look that came into my mother's eyes when I repeated her brother's words to her, and I wished in that moment that I had said nothing, but had kept them to myself. After a moment of silence, during which she seemed to gaze at an object in the distance, she reached and drew me against her side and said in a voice of great sadness, 'Take no notice of him, darling. Your uncle has lived too long on his own.'

I felt my mother's distress that day and, although I knew her answer to be inadequate and evasive, merely a dutiful attempt to reassure me, I did not press her further. Witnessing her distress confirmed my fear, however, that my uncle's charge was not to be lightly dismissed. My mother and I never again approached the subject. It was too fearful. My uncle's suggestion left in me an indelible and tormenting uncertainty about my father's decency which I was never able to speak of to anyone. As the years went by and the war came to an end and we learned the full horror of what had been done, I was not able to rid myself of this tormenting doubt about my father, and it remained between us thereafter until his death, locked in a silent chamber of mutual anxiety and denial that neither of us possessed the courage to breach, for we feared that to breach it would be to end our belief in each other. To this day I possess two unreconciled histories of my father in my imagination—or is it in my memory? One is of a good soldier who leads his men into battle with courage; the other is of a dimly seen figure engaged upon unspeakable acts in a place where the light fails to penetrate. I still experience a chill in my heart whenever I think about this second history. And this chill does not grow weaker with the passage of time, as I once expected it to, but returns to me and comes closer and is stronger as my own end draws nearer, as if its time is approaching. Life, the span of my life I mean, has come to seem to me to be the brief inscription of a circle, the two ends of which are soon to meet, intimate and known to each other all along.

There was a hole in the wall beside my bed in my room under the roof of my uncle's farmhouse. Within this hole I knew there to be another dark place in which violence and human torment were entombed in silence. That it was not a real place but was a place entirely of my own imagination did not weaken its effect upon me, but intensified it. I have never spoken or written of this until setting it down here in my journal alone this night in Dougald Gnapun's house in the abandoned town on the edge of the silent wilderness of featureless scrub. I wonder what influence it is here that liberates me at last to write of these things? From what source do I receive this permission to speak of what has always been for me the unspeakable? I have no doubt that we all harbour within us secret, dark histories of the soul, and that most of us take them to the grave with us, unreconciled and unshared. What consequences might arise for us, we wonder, from turning such imaginary histories into words? We know that to speak of such things is to liberate them from the narrow prison of our own imagination, and that once they are released we cease to be their master and they are seeded in the imagination of everyone who hears of them, and soon they become the common property of our fellows to do with as they will, and then they are changed forever and are no longer ours. My uncle's stories of his legs became mine in this way that night he shared them with me, and it is I who now, alone in this world, give those old legs of his the manner of their continuation, which is not the manner he had of them. And so it is with all shared stories, and has been so since the pitiless Agamemnon was first spoken of.

The hole was roughly circular and, although it was not quite big enough for me to push the first joint of my little finger into, it afforded me the most exquisite nightly terrors. After blowing out my candle each night, I lay in bed under the covers resisting the imaginative attraction of the hole in the wall until I could no longer bear the suspense and was compelled to get up and kneel on my bed and put my eye to the hole, to see if they were still there! A faint draught, chill and damp, breathed upon my eyeball. I knew it to be a breath from another world, and I shivered with the dread expectation it aroused in me. For minutes I knelt there, my eye pressed to the hole, gazing into the impenetrable blackness, until at last I caught the flash of starlight on steel. First I made out one figure, then another, and another, until at last I saw the two vast armies, thousands of creatures, half-human, half-beast, engaged in a silent, bloody and desperate struggle to the death in the country that lay mysteriously beyond my wall.

My imaginary war beyond the wall in my uncle's

farmhouse was a source of far greater dread and excitement to me than the real war that was being fought all over Europe at that time. I knew, of course, that these deformed creatures of my imagination who dwelled beyond the wall were not real, but were aspects of myself mysteriously masked, but the knowledge that they possessed no objective reality did not lessen the terror they inspired in me. My greatest fear each night, a fear which often kept me from sleep for hours, lying rigid between the sheets, was that while I slept these demonic powers would notice the breach in my defences through which I observed them and would make their way through to me and possess me. Worse than this even was my dread that, by a means I dared not contemplate, I would be drawn through the hole into their world while I lay helplessly enthralled in my dreams, and would wake to find myself an exile among them, never to return to this life and to my mother. Once I was among such creatures in their country, I knew, I would not be able to find my way back to this world. Such was, I understood, the iron rule of this fantastic contest. I knew this without needing to inquire how I knew it. My knowing was an intuition. The outcome

of this imaginary war was what I most dreaded; that
vision from my own underworld, the struggle of these
forces, subhuman and terrifying, that were known
only to myself and which I was able to share with no
one. What would happen in the end? I could hardly
bear to think of it. There were no comrades in this
struggle to whom I could look for the reassurance that
I was destined to fight on the side of good. I knew
myself to be alone. And in my solitariness I suffered
the silent doubt of the soul that we suffer as children
when first we begin to know that we are not innocent,
but that it is the common humanity of our species
to be both good and evil. How was it to turn out for
me? What sort of person would I become in the adult
world when I at last took my place in it? To which
side would I belong? To the side of good or to the side
of evil? The answer to this question caused me great
anxiety. I had already failed the gipsy girl's appeal to
my goodness and dreaded that this had marked me
for the other side. I asked myself, had that failure not
been an indication of my essential weakness? As a
young boy I lived in a world of good and evil and my
fear that the forces of evil would win me to their side
was real and was a torment to me. I did not know if I

would have the courage or the strength to withstand the evildoers on the day they at last came to challenge me, as they most assuredly would, the merciless steel of their weapons glinting in the starlight, and I facing them alone, to be proved either the staunch, good man of my longings or the evil man of my greatest dread. Which was it to be? The question haunted me. Which of my father's histories would I become?

It was daylight when I at last put down my pen. I did not attempt to sleep, but set my journal aside on the covers of my bed and got up. I was out in the yard later, after breakfast, shifting the tether peg of the goat, when I heard the car returning. I straightened and turned towards the house, the hammer held in my hand, the peg half-beaten into the ground. The goat and the dogs turned with me; the four of us, dogs, goat and man in the sunlit yard, all turned, looking to where Dougald was getting out of a shiny blue sedan. 'Here's our man back,' I said. He was carrying a black briefcase and was wearing a broad-brimmed black hat and a long black leather coat, which shone like plastic in the sun. His appearance was that of a tall, sombre stranger and I wondered at the world he had just returned from. It was not this world on the edge of the abandoned township. I thought then how little I really knew of his life. He *was* a stranger. He stood watching the blue car reverse down the sideway, then he turned and walked towards the house. His wolf-like bitch came out of the back door. She did not run joyously to meet him, but walked towards him sedately, her head held low and her ears flat, as if she reproached him. This was her first appearance since he had left. She had eaten nothing during his absence. Before going in at the kitchen door, Dougald seemed to recollect himself and he paused and looked towards us. I lifted my hand, the hammer raised in the air—as if I boasted to him of a triumph over some unseen adversary during his absence. He returned my salute, lifting his hand briefly, then turned and went inside.

I was very glad to have him back. With his return the balance of the place, and of my own sanity, seemed at once to be more certain. After a sleepless night in the company of old ghosts from my childhood I was not certain I would remain sane for long if I were to live here alone as he did.

I was walking down the path towards the house from the hen run, carrying the bucket with the eggs in it, when he came out the back door and signalled to me with his mobile telephone. He had taken off his hat and coat and was wearing his familiar faded red-checked shirt and jeans, the sleeves of his shirt buttoned at the wrists as usual. When I drew level with him I said with feeling, 'Welcome home, Dougald. It is really very good to see you.' I would have embraced him, but was too shy to do so. He gave me a slow smile, as if he enjoyed a secret pleasure, knowing in my eyes the ghosts who had haunted my solitary hours during his absence. He handed me the telephone. 'Vita wants to say g'day, old mate.' He turned and went back inside the kitchen and I stood out on the concrete under the tree. She said she was flying north the next day and would spend a week with us before taking me back to Sydney with her. She was not hiring a car this time but expected Dougald and me to meet her at the airport in Mackay. 'Before you go home to Hamburg you can stay here at my place for a few days and I'll show you Sydney properly.' I said it would be wonderful to see her again. My pleasure at the thought of seeing her was genuine, but I also felt a sharp regret that my time alone with Dougald was to come to an end so abruptly. She was so enthusiastic about her visit that I did not feel I could ask her to postpone it, however, and said nothing about my ambivalence. 'I can't wait to get away from this madhouse,' she said. 'It's going to be wicked up there with you guys. Hey listen, we'll go for a picnic to the river. The three of us and the dogs.' It was an idyllic scene she described to me then, our warm, lazy afternoons drifting into evening as we cooked fresh-caught fish over the coals of our fire, and later walked in the moonlit bush together, arm in arm, engaged in animated conversation, as she and I had done as we walked together down Heilwigstrasse that first day of our meeting in Hamburg. There was in her enthusiasm, it seemed to me, an unrealistic expectation of a renewal of that first delight at our surprising friendship. I knew such things could not be repeated and feared her expectation would result in disappointment. Before she hung up she said, 'Make sure Dougald's not late getting in to Mackay. I hate not being met at airports.'

I stood outside the kitchen in the shade of the old tree and looked around me with a feeling of intense regret that I was to take my leave of this place and of Dougald so soon. I felt very strongly in that moment that I had failed to understand what it was I was doing there. I felt I had missed it. That it had evaded me. That I had proved inadequate to it. My silly notion of being on leave from the questions of my life. I felt, as I stood, my dogs pressing their flanks against my legs, that I had been a disappointment. I looked off towards the scrub and I leaned and rubbed the soft ears of the dogs between my fingers. There was, in my friendship with Dougald, surely no sense of an ending but rather of an aborted beginning of something that had not had the opportunity to mature. Vita was certain to take charge the moment she arrived. Her large, energetic presence would bring to an end the peculiar silence of this place. The silence between Dougald and me. *His* silence. A silence that was, in a mysterious way, the medium through which he and I had only just begun to understand each other. 'It's time to go,' I said to the dogs, and picked up the bucket and went into the kitchen.

Dougald was sitting at the table working on his laptop, as if he had not been away, his black briefcase open beside him. He looked up at me as I came in through the door and waited for me to speak. I wanted to tell him that I had no desire to leave just yet. I wanted to thank him while he and I were still on our own. Indeed there was a confusion of emotions in me that I could not hope to express and I could not think how I might speak of my gratitude to him or my fondness for him in a way that would not embarrass us both. I held the bucket for him to see. 'Seven eggs,' I said. Always seven.

8

Landscape of farewell

It was not the light of a passing meteor, nor a dream of youth, nor even the crowing of the rooster, but the barking of the dogs that I woke to. Why is it, I wonder, that I am forever recording my moments of awakening? I assumed Dougald had another early visitor, and I turned over and covered my head with the blanket. The barking persisted, becoming more frenzied by the minute, and I was soon convinced that something must be amiss. I got out of bed and pulled on my dressing-gown and went out to the back door. My two brown dogs pranced excitedly around me, barking and darting out into the yard and back to me again. It was just breaking day, a tight band of cold light splitting the sky in a great arc to the east. I could see no cause for the excitement of the dogs and asked them peevishly why they had woken me so early and had not waited for the rooster to perform his regular office of the day. I was about to return to the warmth of my bed when Dougald and his wolf-like bitch joined us. My dogs became at once subdued and hung close to me.

Dougald was wearing an old denim jacket over his jeans. He glanced at me as if he was surprised to see me there. Murmuring a greeting, he turned and stood looking towards the back of the yard. He was unsmiling, his manner close. I followed the direction of his gaze, and immediately realised the goat was no longer there. I experienced an unpleasant start of guilt at this, recollecting suddenly that I had not finished hammering in her peg the previous day after being distracted by Dougald's arrival in the blue car. Dougald set off, suddenly and without a word, walking with an unusually brisk stride, along the path towards the back of the yard, his bitch close at his side. I and my dogs followed. He went on past the hen run until he reached the back fence, where he stood holding the slack barbed wire and waiting for me to climb through. I thanked him and ducked through the wire. I held it for him in turn and he stepped through after me.

I waited for the dogs to jump through, which they did in such an orderly manner it might have been rehearsed—were we a band of circus performers practising our art at the edge of the town in the magic light of dawn? As we set off across the paddock the hulks of the abandoned bulldozers loomed in the silvery dawn light ahead of us—surely they were not innocent pachyderms after all, but were the abandoned conveyances of a doomed race whose members had all passed away long ago. I was impressed by Dougald's gloomy manner and was anxiously hoping that everything was going to be all right. I knew, however, with that *knowing* we experience at such times, that everything was not going to be all right. Is it not a residue of our childhood dread, this, persisting in us, a superstitious fear of the unknown of the adult world and of the punishment we know we deserve at the hands of our superiors?

Dougald pointed ahead. I looked to where he pointed and at once made out the goat's broken trail through the tussock grass. There were dark patches where her dainty hoofs had wiped the dew, and scuffs where she had dragged her peg across the patches of bare ground. We followed her trail, two men and their dogs walking with purpose across the open paddock in the dawn towards the tall timber lining the riverbank. Surely I had witnessed such a scene somewhere in my past life? An onlooker then, seeing those men and their dogs in the cold light out on some dire business? The air was cold now and Dougald's hands were thrust into the pockets of his old denim jacket, his collar turned up, the closeness of his manner discouraging.

The moment we reached the riverbank we saw her. The ground fell away abruptly at our feet for ten or twelve metres in a near-vertical cliff. It was a dangerous and precipitous place. The elaborate root structures of the great trees had been deeply undermined by erosion, and the mesh of their intricate lattice exposed to the air. Except for a stagnant scum of green algae, which glowed in the cold morning light with a faint and eerie sheen, the riverbed was dry. The exposed tree roots formed the matrix of an elaborate trap. She was hanging by her tether rope, her wooden peg lodged in the fork of a root two or three metres below us. Her tongue lolled from the side of her mouth, purple and swollen, and might have been her disgorged stomach. She hung there, spinning slowly, grinning up at us, her teeth glinting in the rictus of death, her intelligent antique eyes no longer shining with her secret interior life, but bulging blindly, the pupils dull.

She was a hideous sight. Her death must have been slow and terrible, for her hoofs had scored the bank deeply in her helpless struggle to free herself.

I looked at Dougald. He seemed not to be aware of me, and might have been alone there, gazing solemnly down the bank at the strangled goat. Even in that first moment of dismay, before I'd had time to reflect on my reaction to this terrible event, I thought it strange that Dougald did not appear to be surprised, but looked at the dead goat as if her death confirmed something for him— her carcass the fulfilment of a gloomy premonition that had been haunting him forever, a moment long expected, the end of something, not the beginning.

'What can we do?' I said, knowing there was nothing to be done but needing to break the terrible silence between us. So still and inward was he, I might not have spoken. I shivered in the cold morning air and clutched my old grey dressing-gown close around me. I felt accused and shamed by his silence. It was the way I had felt with my uncle when he and I had visited together the scene of a clumsiness of mine that resulted in damage to his new binder. My uncle stood then silently, just as Dougald stood now, looking at his broken machine, his silence more humiliating than if he had shouted or struck me.

I thought sadly what an unhappy pair of old men Vita would find when we fetched her back with us later in the day from the airport at Mackay. Her visit was certain now to be painful and difficult for all of us. How was I to reconcile this sinister riverbank, I wondered, with her romantic fantasy of picnics beside a flowing stream filled with fish? I doubted if she had ever visited this river but had surely only ever imagined it from the distance of Dougald's house, as I had myself. For the first time since my arrival I felt an awkwardness with Dougald, and was no longer confident of his goodwill.

I turned to him and, with a formality that was entirely unworthy of our friendship and the trust he had shown in me, I said, 'Please accept my apology, Dougald. I am truly sorry. This is my fault. I did not take sufficient care to hammer her peg in firmly when I shifted her tether yesterday.' I do not know what I expected him to say to this, but as soon as I had spoken, I heard in the stiffness of my apology an echo of that other apology in the foyer at Warburg Haus—the apology that had postponed my death and had been the beginning of all this.

Dougald turned to me. He looked at me steadily for a long moment, then he said, 'This is not my country.' It took me a moment to realise it was a confession, a revelation of a private truth, and that he required no answer from me. There was in his tone something of a decision, as if his mind had been made up after a period of great uncertainty.

I was incredulous. 'How is this not your country?' I said. What could he mean? It seemed as if he wished to absolve himself from any further connection to the gruesome sight below us, and even to dissociate himself from his entire situation in this place with this astonishing statement. With a small lift of his shoulders, which I took to be the gesture of a man who feels himself defeated—though whether by some internal incapacity of his own or by external circumstances and the inadequacies of others, I could not say—he said, 'We'd better get going, or we'll be late for Vita.' He turned abruptly and set off across the paddock back towards the house.

I stood watching him go. The enormous silence of the landscape was suddenly close and oppressive, the unrelieved solitude of the forlorn township in the ocean of scrub, the abandoned machines rusting into the ground, the mean little fibro house; suddenly it was not a haven but a scene of desolation and failure, and Dougald a bewildered exile in it. I would have given anything to have been able to go back and hammer in the goat's peg firmly. It felt to me as if it had been only the surety of her tether that had kept our expectations alive. I turned again to the riverbank, as if I expected her to be gone and for this to be nothing more than a momentary confusion of the senses. She revolved slowly in the grey light, displayed in her death agony as if she were the victim of a barbaric fetish, a warning to travellers. I felt once again that old sense of moral failure and I thought of the gipsy girl and her fruitless appeal to me. I saw her this time, however, not in a real scene recollected from memory, but in an imaginary setting imbued with the nostalgia of my youthful longing to one day grow up to be a good man. She walked away from me across a field in the soft light of a summer evening, and I was young again and I followed her, for there was a modest invitation in the way she paused and turned to look back at me, smiling her knowing, solitary smile, gazing at me from a landscape of farewell.

9

Encounter with a fellow countryman

We were sitting at the kitchen table eating our breakfast. I had developed a headache and had no appetite for the food. I pushed my plate away and sat back and looked out the door towards the tree. I remember the moment with such clarity I believe I could still count the bars of sunlight and shadow cast by the shed and the cottage across the trunk of that ancient eucalypt. As I sat looking out on the familiar scene, squinting against the light and the throbbing in my head, I asked myself, *Why this depth of desolation?* I was moved by love and sorrow for this place, and for the strange and sudden loss of it—my failure. My failure. That is how I saw it. How else was

I to see it? What would Vita say? What would I say to her? I have rarely felt so useless to my fellow creatures. It should have been me hanging by that rope, not the innocent nanny-goat.

Dougald was sitting beside me, as we always sat for our meals, the two of us side by side facing the open door—as if we resolutely faced together whatever the day was to bring—but separated now by our own thoughts. The newspapers and old magazines and periodicals were pushed into an untidy pile on the far side of the table to make room for our plates. He paused in his eating and lifted his head, pointing with his fork through the wall of the kitchen in the direction of the highway, and he said in a voice that was easy and conversational, 'Her mother was a road kill.'

I wondered for an instant who he could be talking about.

'Vita picked her up out there two years ago. She was sitting by the mother's carcass on the highway. The little thing was hardly strong enough to stand when Vita brought her in.' He looked at me. 'She bottle-fed her for weeks.' He lifted his chin. 'There, in your bedroom.' He folded a piece of bacon with his fork, put it in his mouth and chewed, looking off thoughtfully through the wall. 'There's hundreds of them wild goats out there in the scrub.'

I said miserably, 'I would give anything to bring her back to life.'

He said in a matter-of-fact way, as if it were a long-held belief, 'Nothing's ever going to work out up this way.'

I looked at him with surprise. But he offered no more, and might have believed he had pronounced a sufficient sense of his own fate, and an explanation of our situation, with these few words—the fault not in my failings nor in the death of the goat, nor yet in himself, but in the sterile equation of his exile, *up this way*. The air trembled with the distant thunder of the mine. It was as if a great wave approached us. I made up my mind then. 'I'll get the plane down to Sydney from Mackay today,' I said.

He said nothing for a minute or two, but went on eating. Then he said mildly, and as if it were more an observation than a question, 'You won't be spending the week here with Vita, then?'

'I think it's time for me to go home.'

We sat side by side at the kitchen table saying nothing, the remains of our breakfast in front of us, looking out at the sunlit tree and the yard, the cottage and the shed with the old red truck, the two brown dogs watching from the concrete. We might have just received news that the battle had been lost. There did seem to have been a battle. And wasn't it our dismay at finding ourselves on the losing side of it that had rendered us mute? For this was not our old easy silence. I knew well enough from the common experience of my generation that how we are to speak of defeat is less obvious to us than how we might boast of our heroism and our glorious victories. No doubt Dougald and I were both asking ourselves how it was we had come so badly out of this, when we surely had believed ourselves to be carrying the day with honour. And to this question we had no answer. Defeat is a great silencer. To explain it we must accuse ourselves, or we must lie.

He pushed back his chair and got to his feet. He walked across the kitchen and went into his bedroom. A moment later he came out and set a thick volume on the table in front of me. 'This old feller was a German too.' He stood looking down at the book, then turned and crossed the floor to his bedroom again. Before he went in he paused with his hand to the door and gestured at the book on the table in front of me. 'You can read it later. We'd better get ready.' He grinned, his features suddenly lighting up with his customary cheerfulness. 'Young Miss

Vita hates people being late to meet her. That girl likes the welcoming committee to show up on time. She's not going to be impressed when you tell her you're heading home.' He held the door to let the bitch go in ahead of him, her claws tapping on the boards, then he followed her and closed the door. A moment later I heard the murmur of his voice. I guessed he was talking on the telephone. By the way the volume of his voice was rising I supposed him to be arguing with Vita.

I drew the book towards me. It was a nineteenth-century volume. Its covers and spine were missing, the binder's stitches exposed, knotted with expert fingers long ago and still holding good. On the reverse of the first page, facing the title page, there was a steel engraving of a broad prospect of lake and mountains. Two men reclined on the grass in the foreground beside a smoking fire and observed with keen interest a flight of birds that was crossing the sky in the centre of their view. The title page read: *Journal of an Overland Expedition in Australia from Moreton Bay to Port Essington, a Distance of Upwards of 3000 Miles, During the Years 1844–1845, by Dr Ludwig Leichhardt.* So that was it, another German traveller in Australia. The date of publication was 1847. To have travelled three thousand miles across Australia at that time must have been a venture sustained by the most passionate of visions and an intemperate and rare persistence. Between Leichhardt's name and the publisher's imprint at the bottom of the page, there was an epigraph. It was a quotation from Goethe's *Iphigenie auf Tauris*—Iphigenie, daughter of the god-like Agamemnon, that most merciless of warriors. Seeing Goethe's familiar lines, I felt something of the poignant enchantment, indeed it is a kind of sadness, that we experience when we meet a fellow countryman in a foreign land far away from our own and know, suddenly, that it is ourselves who are the exotic objects in that landscape. This was the only real book I had seen in Dougald's possession. I read the two lines aloud, filling the kitchen with the sound of my native tongue and making the dogs sit up and prick their ears at the strangeness of it—as if they thought I was casting a spell. 'Die Götter brauchen manchen guten Mann/Zu ihrem Dienst auf dieser weiten Erde.' I felt very keenly at that moment the pointlessness of my entire existence on this earth.

Dougald came out of his bedroom and began gathering his papers and putting them in his briefcase. He was wearing the black felt hat and the leather overcoat, his travelling costume. I watched him. He was a big man, tall and sombre, his complexion dark, his bold features filled with the shadows and crevices of his anxieties. He was an impressive figure. I greatly admired him and felt, suddenly, the privilege of his friendship. At my age one does not expect new friends. Now I had two, and was about to lose them both. He straightened and looked across at me. 'You'd better get your skates on, old mate,' he said. I felt with him then as I had felt with Vita in Hamburg, when she had been going home. I knew I was going to miss him greatly and that he had left me with a question about myself that without him I would never be able to solve.

'Let me read you this,' I said. I read Goethe's lines to him in German, then I offered my translation. 'The gods need many a good man at their service in this wide world.' The words seemed to apply to him as he stood there before me in his long coat and his black hat, a man surely directed by his conscience and his love towards the recovery of the broken realities of his people. 'It is from Goethe's great drama of exile,' I said.

He considered a moment, his lips pursed. 'It sounds better in German,' he said.

It is what we most desire, to share with another the inexpressible solitude of our knowledge of ourselves. He was right. Goethe sounds best in German.

He set his briefcase on the table and gestured at the book. 'We carried that old book around with us everywhere when we went out on our researches in the old days. We're in there,' he said, making the claim confidently. 'The highways and villages of our Old People. Leichhardt set it all down just the way he saw it. There's information in that book we could not have recovered by any other means.' He laughed softly, but I think not because he was amused. 'It's yours,' he said. 'Take it back to Hamburg with you.'

'No!' I objected. 'I can't possibly accept such a generous gift. You will need it when you go out on your researches again.'

'When's that going to be? I don't think I'll be going out on too many of them. But if I do, I promise you I'll come over there to Hamburg and get that book back off you.' He looked at me and said steadily, 'Take it. It will be a reminder to you.'

10

The miracle of the yellow robin

Dougald's old red truck bounded over the corrugated surface of the road at a surprising speed, its shock absorbers, like the knees of old men, no longer absorbing the shocks but delivering them to our spines. We had left the town behind some while ago and were travelling along the wide gravel road that Vita and I had come in along those three weeks earlier. I did not remember it. To either side of us the unbroken drift of low grey scrub. We saw no other vehicles and when Dougald's mobile telephone rang he did not pull over to the verge to answer the call but stopped on the crown of the road, at which our following dust rolled over us, as if the sky darkened. Vita's voice was loud and aggrieved. There was a crisis in her department and she was needed. Dougald grimaced at the loudness of her voice and held the telephone inches from his ear. I could hear Vita's every word, Dougald discreetly murmuring his responses. She was not on the plane to Mackay but was in her office at the university preparing to go into a meeting. 'This trip's just never going to work out,' she yelled. Where had I heard this phrase before? I wondered why I did not feel surprised. Our dust drifted slowly over the low scrub. I got out of the truck and walked to the side of the road.

Standing in the cool morning air was a relief from the pounding in the cabin of the truck, and I was glad to be in contact with the place. I did not really want to leave. There was a delicate spiciness in the air. I could see that the surface of the ground within the scrub was a grey hardpan and was littered with dried leaves and twigs, as if someone had gone around scattering them there to make it look real. The small trees and shrubs were so densely grown I had to search for a place where I could gain access. The branches yielded easily, however, when I pushed against them, bending and swaying with the movement of a curtain. I had soon penetrated fifteen or twenty paces into the scrub, my footfalls crunching lightly on the dry ground cover. I stopped and looked back the way I had come. I could not see Dougald's truck or the road. Had I arrived at this place from within the interior, as Leichhardt and his party must have done had they come this way, I would not have suspected the existence of a road only a few metres away. The sense of concealment and solitude was perfect. I stood in the perfumed silence and looked about me, charmed by this unlikely other world so enclosed within itself and hidden from the outside. I was standing there listening, as if I expected to hear something, when a small bird landed on a trembling twig a few inches in front of me. I held my breath. The exquisite little creature examined me curiously with its tiny black eyes. It was the size of the European robin; its breast, however, was not red but a rich cadmium yellow that glowed from within the shadows of its perch. The bird observed me without fear, the two of us regarding each other with a kind of wonder. Suddenly the yellow robin was gone. I had entered its magical world. There was a serenity, untroubled and modest, within the shelter of the scrub that was at once calming, reassuring and strangely familiar. I could easily have belonged there. There was something akin to memory in my recognition of it, quite as if I had been there at an earlier period of my life, or in another life altogether. How many lives do we have? But I am no kind of resurrectionist.

The dry crunching of a step behind me made me turn. Dougald was making his way towards me, the mobile telephone held to his ear, his outstretched arm brushing aside the branches of the low trees and shrubs. He came up to me and handed me the telephone. 'Vita wants a word, old mate.'

I took the telephone from him and held it to my ear. 'So you're not coming up to see us after all?' I said. But she did not want to talk about her aborted trip.

'I met someone,' she said, imparting a secret.

'Is he the black prince?'

'This feller's not what I had in mind, Max.'

'But you like him?'

'He's a whitefella.'

'I see,' I said, although I was not sure that I did see.

'I want to know what you think of him.'

I wondered if Dougald had told her about the death of her goat.

She said, 'That's not all.'

I could not see Dougald and supposed that he had gone back to the truck.

'He's an academic. I can't seem to get away from them.

I just feel so good when I'm with him, Max. We never stop laughing. It sounds so bloody clichéd! What I want to know is, what am I going to do when the black prince does show up? It scares me. What am I going to do with my little Brian then?'

I smiled to think of her dilemma. 'Keep them both.'

'It's not funny! Don't laugh at me! I love the little guy. There's nothing to him. Honestly, wait till you see him. His shoulders are narrower than mine. D'you reckon that's all right, for the bloke to be narrower than the girl? And what's this shit Dougald tells me about you heading home?'

Her abrupt switch took me by surprise. I replied carefully, 'I was going home with you anyway.'

'That wasn't settled.'

'This is only a week sooner. It's time for me to leave, Vita.'

She said, 'You're making a run for it.'

'That's nonsense.'

'You're a disappointment!'

'I know. I'm sorry.'

'What happened?'

'Dougald didn't tell you?'

'You tell me.'

I cleared my throat. 'I'm sorry, Vita. But I'm afraid I accidentally caused the death of your goat.'

She said nothing.

'I'm sorry,' I said.

'Fuck you, Max!' she said quietly.

'I'm sorry.'

'That poor little bugger. Jesus! What happened?'

I told her.

'You're hopeless. You're not to be trusted.'

'I'm sorry.'

'Don't keep saying you're fucking sorry! This is not why you're running out on Dougald.'

'I'm not running out on Dougald.'

'He needs a mate to get him out and about or he's not going to last the distance. I've told you that. What happened to the idea that you'd talk him into showing you his country? You're running out on him. Face it. He needs you. But he's never going to say so. He's too proud to do that. You don't know anything about that man.' She was silent. Then she said, 'This could be your last chance. Have you thought of that?'

'I'm an old man.'

'Don't start that old man shit, Max! Have enough respect for me not to make pathetic excuses for yourself!'

Neither of us spoke for some time.

She said seriously, 'I loved that little nanny-goat.'

'I'm sorry.'

'I hope you gave her a decent burial.'

I said nothing. An image in my mind of the goat's hideous carcass spinning slowly above the green slime in the stagnant pool accused me of failing my friends.

When she spoke again she was being quieter and more persuasive. 'Promise me you'll sleep on it, Max.'

I said, 'I'm packed and on my way.'

'This is me, Vita, who's asking you. Remember me? I'm the reason you're here. If it wasn't for me you'd be six feet under in bloody Hamburg. You owe me for the nanny-goat too. And you owe Dougald. Don't argue! I know what I'm talking about. I'm asking you to think about this. Promise me you'll sleep on it, just for one night. Then, if you still want to go, well just go. Will you promise?'

I always seemed to have to promise her something. We were back at the airport in Hamburg.

Dougald called to me from the road, 'You all right in there, old mate?'

I called back that I was still talking with Vita.

'Remember what you said to me in front of those PhD

students?' she said. 'I was impressed. You apologised to me for betraying my generation. For doing second-rate work. That's what you said. I thought that was pretty good. I said then I'd ask you one of these days why you did that. So I'm asking you now, why did you do it? What was the point of apologising if you weren't going to change your ways and make amends? Come on, Max, I'm asking you, for Christ's sake. Why fucking apologise unless you meant to reform yourself?'

The yellow robin settled on a branch inches from my face, as if it needed to satisfy itself that the apparition had been real. Having satisfied itself that I was really there, it proceeded to ignore me. It turned its head quickly this way then that, then it pounced on something on the ground and flew off, the tiny legs of an insect sticking from its bill like whiskers.

'Do I get an answer or what?'

I said, 'I apologised to you that day because I knew Winifred would have approved.'

'And she's going to approve of you making a run for it now?'

When I did not reply she said, 'It's not my generation you'll be betraying if you make a run for it. It's Winifred. The trust you two guys had between you all those years.

Your life and hers, your love for each other, the point of it all. Hey Max? That's what you'll be betraying. The point of it all. I have to go. You'd just better be sure this is the way you want it to end between you and Dougald. You'd just better be sure of that, Max. That guy loves you. Sleep on it tonight and give me a call in the morning and let me know what you've decided. I'll accept your decision. I won't argue. Okay? Will you promise me, please, Max? Just one night. It won't kill you.'

'All right,' I said. 'Okay. I promise.'

'Thanks, Max. I've got to go now. Call me tomorrow.'

Dougald was sitting in the truck with the radio playing country and western music. I handed him the telephone. 'I'm not going to Mackay today,' I said.

He switched off the radio and started the engine. He chuckled. 'I didn't think you would be.'

'Well you were right.'

He grinned and swung the truck around and started back towards Mount Nebo.

The red road unrolling under us, the cloudless blue of the sky above. I asked him, 'What did you mean when you said this is not your country?'

He lifted a hand from the wheel and pointed across the ocean of scrub towards the south and without the least hesitation, as if I'd asked him what time of the day it was, he said, 'My country's over in them escarpments in that old Expedition Range.'

I said, 'So why do you live here? Why don't you go back and live there?'

'We're working on it, old mate. We'll get there. These things take their own time.'

I said, 'I should like to see your country, if there is an opportunity to do so before I go home.'

He turned and looked at me. 'That would be good, old mate. Real good. I'd like to show her to you.'

11

A decent burial

I dreamed I watched a horse kill its rider, and the horse looked back at me, its eye fierce and triumphant, the man's torn and bloodied corpse twisted and awry beneath its hoofs. I knew it to be a horse though it possessed the features of my uncle. I was afraid of it with a child's fear. The dream woke me and I lay in my bed shaken by the violence of it. I could not get back to sleep, and I sat up and put on my light. I resolved to write an account of the events of the day in my journal, in the hope that I would bring myself to an understanding of my true place in this affair of Vita and Dougald, and would perhaps begin to find my way by this means to a resolution of the uncertainties of my own existence—if such an ambition were not entirely ridiculous.

When I took up my pen, however, I was scarcely able to compose the simplest of sentences. I wrote a sentence then crossed it out and sat a while, then wrote another and looked at it. But it too made little sense to me and I crossed it out also. There was a stubborn silence in me that refused to yield up my emotions and my thoughts in words. My subject was closed to me. Why? It was as if my mind—my unconscious, I suppose I must say—had decided that this thing was not to be written but that something else was required from me on this occasion. Not writing, but action. It was not a time for words. But what action lay open to me?

I put my pen and my journal aside and got out of bed. It was my intention to make a cup of tea and to read Leichhardt's *Journal* in order to bring calm into my mind. Dougald snored steadily in the next room, an engine of contentment. Despite his exile, he seemed certain of his universe and of his place within it. I envied him his untroubled sleep. I put on my dressing-gown and my slippers and went out into the kitchen. The back door was open to the night as usual. The great old tree hung in the frame of the doorway as if it were a theatre backdrop, its limbs black against the luminous sky. I was glad to see it again. There was a sense of privilege in standing there. My two brown dogs came and stood at the threshold and looked with me into the night. I remembered Vita saying, with a certain degree of trust that had shamed me, *I hope you gave her a decent burial.* And at once I saw the strangled goat hanging above the river out there in the moonlight where we had abandoned her to the scavengers, to the eaters of carrion who would find her there. She had surely not deserved that. I stepped out into the yard and stood beneath the tree, attending to the wonderful silence. The night vibrated with the stillness of outer space. I had no plan, but was moved by the need to do something. Cautiously I stepped along the path, careful to make no sudden noise in case I disturbed the rooster, who would be certain to crow to the moon if woken. As I walked along the path an after-image of the merciless eye of the horse touched my mind with its passionate horror.

I grew uneasy as I climbed through the slack wire of the back fence into the paddock. Being alone in the night in this place made me a trespasser, I knew that. My dogs kept me close company, staying at my heels as if they too felt this unease of trespass. I walked past the looming hulks of the abandoned bulldozers—dreary objects to the mind—and went on across the incline of the paddock, the silver grass shining in the moonlight, until we came to the river. I stood on the bank looking over the sheer fall of the cliff.

She hung below us just as Dougald and I had left her. She was still now, no longer revolving slowly at the end of her tether, a dark weight above the gleaming pool of phosphorescent algae. It was little more than two metres from where I stood on the bank to the point below me where her peg was caught among the exposed roots. I could see no way of reaching across the gap, however. I searched around among the fallen limbs at the base of the tree for a stick. I soon found one and lay down on the bank and reached with it to the full stretch of my arm. The end of the stick just touched the peg but I could do nothing with it. I threw it aside and found a longer one. I managed to force the point under the peg where it was lodged in the roots, but the moment I put a little strain on it the end of the stick snapped off. The dead weight of the goat's carcass had locked the peg firmly in its trap. I stood looking down at her. I could see that it might just be possible for me to climb down and release the peg with my bare hands. Such a manoeuvre looked difficult, and even dangerous, for it was quite a drop to the stagnant pool, but it did not look impossible. If I were careful, surely I would be able to use the lattice of the roots as a ladder. When I was a boy on my uncle's farm I would not have hesitated for an instant before attempting such a feat. Now I recalled the iron bar in the cottage and I doubted if I still possessed sufficient strength in my arms to hold my own weight. If Vita could hear my thoughts she would no doubt have accused me of using old age as an excuse for my cowardice. It was an accusation that did not seem quite fair to me.

I stood looking down at the goat for some time, hesitating and uncertain. It was true and was not an empty excuse for cowardice. I no longer enjoyed the confidence of youth. Everything I contemplated these days was hedged about with these pathetic hesitations. Vita had scoffed at me for claiming the excuse of old age, but it is easy to scoff when you are young and have not yet felt the pains and the failings that plague our bodies and our minds when old age arrives. When that happens we know ourselves to be the victims of a sudden disease for which there is no cure. The irony was, surely, that I almost certainly despised my faltering even more than she did. The onset of old age seemed unjust to me and I was often angered by it, wanting nothing more than to revolt against it and to rid myself of it and return to my former state. Indeed I sometimes almost believed, in moments of utter self-delusion, that I would recover from this temporary setback and return to full health and vigour one day, as if old age were nothing more serious or lasting than a tiresome dose of the flu. I had been youthful all my life, after all, and youthfulness was the condition I was accustomed to, not this trembling infirmity.

It would have been reasonable at this point to have returned to the house and to have waited until Dougald was awake, when I might have enlisted his assistance. But there was a stubbornness in me that night insisting I release the goat unaided and give her a proper burial, an aim which had by now become my ambition. It was my responsibility alone. There is surely an element of madness in all of us, which at times refuses to yield to the sadness of mere reason. That moonlit night on the bank of the Nebo River, I knew that according to the irresistible laws of this madness, laws which are little different to the laws of literature and myth, the challenge before me was mine in the solitary and heroic sense of such deeds and could not be shared with someone else and remain a true act of contrition. Was that it then? An act of contrition? Was I humiliating myself out here in the night of the Australian wilderness because I was troubled in my spirit by a sense of guilt? I suppose I was, or at least that such a sense was partly my reason for this. I had regrets, after all, that gave me sufficient reason to be troubled in my spirit.

I drew the belt of my dressing-gown tight around my waist and knotted it, then I lay down close against the rough bark of the great tree and, clutching a knobby protuberance at its base, edged out over the drop along the principal root, feeling my way backwards into the horrid darkness above the pool with my slippered feet. The root curved out strongly from the base of the tree and for the first two metres or so remained almost horizontal. As it reached out into space, getting further from the tree, however, it began to dip more steeply, until it branched into two just above the peg, by which time it was pointing almost straight down into the void. At this point its separate limbs were joined by the trellis of other smaller intersecting roots. I felt foolish lying there on the root in the moonlight and may even have laughed out loud. Certainly a detached intelligence in me observed these antics of the old man with a superior scorn from the safety of the bank, where the dogs had stayed. As always, there were two of us, the I who did the thing and the superior other within who stood aside and commented on the doing of it. Why is it that this other within is always younger and better informed and more critical than the I who is required to engage with the unyielding facts of reality?

It was an impossible thing to have attempted. But the further I went, the bolder and more justified I felt myself to be in attempting it, and the more worthy I felt myself to be. To be worthy. And to be a fool. I was afraid, to be sure, but surely I was not a coward. I eased myself out along the root until I reached a point where, if I were to continue, I would have to let go of my handhold on the tree. I stopped at this point, lying along the narrow root and clinging to the tree with my outstretched hand, the emptiness of the drop into the dark pool beneath me, my weight drawn downwards by the increasing curvature of the root, which had begun to sag under me. In order to progress further with my plan I needed to let go of the knobbly protuberance at the base of the tree, but I found that my fear of falling was too great and I could not open my fingers and release my hold. My faithless observing other reminded me, in his always faintly scoffing voice, how Katriona had stubbornly resisted Winifred and me in just this way on many occasions when she was a small child, and how we had been forced to prise open her fingers in order to make her relinquish her grip on some toy or other, or from the seat of a swing in a park when we told her it was time to leave and to go home and have a bath. It was more in revolt against the derision of this inner voice than innate courage that spurred me to snatch my hand away from the tree. 'There!' I cried, and sent a hysterical laugh into the uncaring night that drew an astonished bark from the dogs. I was now clinging to the root with both arms wrapped tightly around it.

Once I no longer had a steadying grip on the tree I experienced the greatest difficulty retaining my balance, and I swayed back and forth above the blackness, the flexing of the root seeming to increase dramatically with this loosening of my attachment to the bank. I felt myself to be on a springboard of the kind one sees at public swimming baths. Too afraid to move any further out along the root, I clung there in the moonlight like a giant insect that has found a place in which to undergo the transformation of its pupation. During my struggle my slippers had fallen soundlessly from my feet into the pool below. I looked up and met the eyes of my dogs, who lay side by side on their bellies above me, their heads and forepaws over the bank, wriggling and whimpering, as if they would have joined me had they possessed the foolhardiness to attempt the leap.

Providing I did not attempt any further movement I knew myself to be in no immediate danger of falling. There was also no imperative for a further development of my plan of action just yet. The night air was soft and cool and I was warmed by my exertions and was not too uncomfortable. I remembered lying for hours along the branch of an old chestnut tree on my uncle's farm one endless summer day of my solitary childhood, dreaming of life, no doubt, or what in my imagination then passed for life. Now that I was lying perfectly still I noticed a small rhythmic movement of the root. My struggles had set the carcass of the goat below me swinging from side to side with the motion of a pendulum, causing my root to sway gently back and forth. I rested my cheek against the cool wood and closed my eyes. I would rest a while before attempting my next move.

A moment later I opened my eyes. The toes of my left foot were touching the goat's peg! I was sure of it. I recognised the slim tapering form of the peg that I had hammered into the ground a number of times. And, yes, there was the knotted rope! I explored the peg and the knot blindly with my toes and realised that if I could hook my foot under the peg and, by bending my knee, slowly rotate it upwards towards me, I could probably release it. I had barely begun the manoeuvre when the trap let go with a vicious snap. The carcass of the goat plummeted to the river below and the recoil of the root, released from her weight, clamped my foot in a vice-like grip. The pain was fierce. I cried out and involuntarily drew myself downwards towards my trapped foot. As my foot rotated several degrees, a movement caused by the levering action of my upper leg as I drew myself downwards, the root released me as suddenly as it had gripped me, like a bow releasing an arrow. I yelled with fear and pain and swung about helplessly, hanging vertically now above the pool, my weight on my extended arms. I sobbed and hung on. I did not possess the strength to drag myself back up the root and regain the bank. The only thing would be to let myself slip down the root a little at a time and to drop the final three or four metres into the stagnant pool, where the carcass of the goat no doubt floated belly up in the moonlight beneath me.

Crying out with the fierce pain in my shoulders and ankle, I endeavoured to let myself slip down the root inch by inch, but I did not have sufficient strength in my arms and with a howl of fear and pain I fell through the tangle of roots into the darkness.

12

Winifred's naked shoulders

So here I am sitting up in bed again—it is an image from which I am finding it difficult to escape. It is the apartment on Schlüterstrasse, and I am reading an article in some journal or other which is revisiting, with a certain wit and imagination, Orloff's 1936, *Bismarck und Katherina Orloff*, a book of my father's day which, among other delights, offers an account of the romantic love of a young woman of twenty-two for a man of fifty.

Winifred comes into the bedroom and begins to undress. Winifred always undresses at the foot of our bed in front of the dressing-table mirror. While she takes off her clothes she glances at herself from time to time in the mirror. At fifty Winifred is still a handsome and sexually interesting woman. I have often observed, with a small thrill of jealousy, how men much younger than she look at her with admiration. Her bare arms and shoulders in the soft lamplight of the bedroom are as exciting to me as they were when we first met. Winifred is a woman who has matured into her beauty. Although she was scarcely more than twenty when we first met, she had not been, as Bismarck's Kathi Orloff was, *pretty, irresponsible and gay*, but was a rather serious young woman. Most people, I think, would probably not have described her as beautiful at that age. She became beautiful later, and people who knew her only when she was young were surprised when they met the woman of beauty and distinction Winifred grew into later in life.

I saw her beauty, however, from the first moment. I was in my early thirties when we first met. I was coming down the central staircase at the university library and she was standing at the index boxes on the lower floor going through cards, bending forward to make a note, then straightening again. There was something so lovely in the way she moved her shoulders, her dark hair falling forward over her face, that it made me catch my breath. Entranced, I stood on the landing of the stairs and watched her until at last, feeling my gaze on her, she looked up and saw me. For more than thirty years we were happy together . . .

While she undresses at the foot of the bed, she is telling me about something that happened to one of her colleagues at work during the day, and she removes her clothes in a preoccupied and unselfconscious way, her attention caught up in the telling of her story. I am not really listening to her story, but am admiring her. I pretend that I am not present, and that she is a woman alone in the privacy of her bedroom, or even the bedroom of her lover. There is in this subterfuge an element of trespass and of the forbidden that I find attractive and enticing. This woman who I am watching undress is not my wife, the mother of my daughter, my friend and companion of thirty years, but is a stranger, a woman I desire and whose nakedness I have never before seen.

With care, slowly, she takes her clothes off and places them on the low tub chair beside the dressing table, raising her arms, leaning and bending; then, when she is naked at last, she stands before the dressing table and removes her jewellery. It is only now, finally, that our eyes meet in the mirror. It is an exquisite moment. In the middle of a lecture at the university one morning I paused midway through a sentence at the sudden intrusion of this image of Winifred standing naked at the foot of our bed, her arms raised to unclasp her beads, our eyes meeting in the dressing-table mirror. I fell silent, my notes on Innocent III forgotten as I gazed at the image of my beautiful wife, and my spirits lifted with the certainty that I would see her again that night, and no doubt I smiled stupidly at my bemused students . . .

It is this moment, this image, that stands at the centre of our erotic life. This is the portal through which Winifred and I are transported to that other world of our sexuality, an enchanted landscape beyond the commonplace of our day. After being together for thirty years we no longer make love every night, of course, but often read or talk of our concerns about the tedious life Katriona is living in London with her unpleasant husband, or discuss our plans for travelling, or we speak of our work or the news we have seen on television that night, the massacres and famines. But when we do make love, it is for me always with these soft lamplit images of Winifred's naked shoulders and arms, and the lovely hollow of her back, in my mind. To this day, making love with her astonishes me. Naked in each other's arms she and I cease to be the everyday companions of our lives, those people whom we know so well, whom we care for and love so dearly, and whom we hate fiercely in moments of pure insanity, but are transformed into the perfect strangers of our erotic desires. During the day we never discuss the lives and times of these perfect strangers to whom we give ourselves so passionately and with such greedy abandon, crying out with voices that are not our own and do not belong to our daily selves. These secret strangers never meet as familiars during our daily lives. The human and natural tragedies that are reported every day on the television and in the newspapers, and which preoccupy and often dominate our conversation during dinner and at the breakfast table, do not exist for these other beings whom we meet only at night under cover of darkness. It has always been so, from the very beginning, from that first day of bliss that began for us in the university library when she and I looked at each other and held our breath with the certain expectation of what must follow from such a meeting. From that first day we have lived our erotic lives outside the history of our time, in a perpetual present. On all quotidian subjects these secret erotic selves remain silent, as if such knowledge, such a mixing of one with the other, would erode the power of the spell under which we each cast the other. Naked in bed at night together we are released from the real world of the everyday and become the subjects of a power that we do not understand. It is the greatest power we know. It is the source of our joy. It is our most sacred place. We never discuss it, either with each other or with anyone else . . .

The bright light of dawn burst through my closed lids suddenly and drew me up from the depths and I opened my eyes. The light blinded me and I turned my head away and groaned and closed my eyes again. *She was gone! The darkness was only darkness!* 'She is dead,' I cried, stricken. And I heard my voice as if it was the voice of another, a desperate and a forlorn man who has lost his reason to live. Without her I am blind and dead too . . .

I heard Dougald speak then, or curse, but I did not understand him. I opened my eyes again and looked up. He pushed his torch into his pocket and leaned and grasped me under the arms and dragged me from the edge of the pool and out of the mud onto the dry bed of the river. He bent over me, his features inverted so that he seemed to grimace at me in the cold dawn light, the great purple pouches under his eyes sagging and his cheeks puffed out, his breathing hard and laboured. Pain and grief washed through me and I cried out. He knelt beside me and cradled my head in his arms, holding me to him and murmuring words of comfort. My two brown dogs were licking my hands. Then I remembered the fall. The anguish of my loss washed through me like a violent poison and I wept and called her name aloud. She was gone. My Winifred was gone and would never come back. I had lost her forever. How was I to endure without her?

13

The storyteller

The days of my convalescence passed pleasantly. Dougald
bound my ankle and made me stay in bed. I did not resist.
He was a capable nurse and I was not in great pain. In a
way it was a relief to give up all resistance and to lie back
and let him take care of me. He, too, seemed changed
by my altered state. Once I had been immobilised,
propped in bed against my pillows, and was no longer
threatening to run off to Hamburg, he began to talk to
me. I was content to listen. I was more than content;
I was intrigued by what he had to tell me. Now that he
had begun to speak he spoke well and without hesitation
of the things that most concerned him. It was agreeable,

indeed restful, to be diverted from my own troubles and to learn something of the sum of his.

He stood beside my bed looking out the window along the road. 'Winter's coming,' he said, no doubt seeing some subtle change in the look of things. It was the season, he said, that everyone waited for; the dry, cool season, with frosts in the mornings and a need for fires in the evenings, the days windless and warm, the sky a soft blue without clouds. As he spoke he moved his large hands about with ample gestures, describing the things he spoke of, lingering at my window as if he possessed all the time in the world—which no doubt he did. He brought me a breakfast of toast, two soft-boiled eggs and a mug of tea and stood at the window watching the empty road that we had returned along, his presence filling my room.

'You'll be fit enough to walk on that in three weeks.' He said this with the authority of a man who had lived his life without doctors, in situations where sprains and broken bones were commonplace. 'She was the decoy, old mate,' he said, and smiled down at me, watching me scoop at the innards of an egg. 'It was you they were after.' I looked up at him, realising only when I saw the amusement in his eyes that he spoke of the goat. It was his judgment on the affair. I did not ask him who *they* were. The fates, no doubt, or some equivalent of those blind forces that interrupt the ordered course of our lives and set us on paths we have not wilfully chosen to follow. That I had possessed the capacity to have behaved in such an erratic way that night, obedient apparently to an inner force that was neither rational nor sane, seemed to have greatly reassured him. My dependence on him too, it was plain, pleased him no end and seemed to have been the thing that had liberated in him the confidence to speak to me of himself.

One evening, a few days after the accident, he did not watch the television after his meal as usual but came into my room with a box of wood and lit a fire in the brick hearth. He brought a chair with him and when he had lit the fire he sat on the chair tending it. I had been reading Leichhardt's *Journal* and I set it aside on the box beside my bed. I was glad of his company and was expecting something from him. He said nothing for some time, but looked across at me once or twice, acknowledging the homeliness of our situation. The wolf-like bitch did not come into my room with him, but lay across the threshold, her head on her paws, her disapproving gaze on her master. My brown dogs were camped beneath us under the floorboards in the dust. This was our small family, reduced—indeed, brought together—by the death of the beautiful nanny-goat. At length Dougald turned from tending the fire and said, 'You're going to be laid up here for a while with nothing to do, old mate.'

I reached and touched the book lying beside my journal and Winifred's photograph on the box beside my bed. 'I shall read Leichhardt,' I said.

He considered the book. 'I think you'll soon run through that.' He looked at me. 'Then what will you do?'

'I don't know,' I said. 'I may reread it. All good books are better at the second reading.' He seemed to wait for me. 'Is there something you would like me to do?' I asked him.

He indicated my journal with a small fling of his hand. 'You keep a diary.'

'It is my journal,' I said. 'I don't write in it every day. It is not really a diary.'

'Have you written about the nanny?'

'No.'

'Will you?'

'Is that what you want me to write?'

He laughed. 'Do you think you *will* write the story of your night with Vita's little goat?' he asked. 'It would be an amusing thing to read.'

'I've not thought of doing so. I don't think Vita would be amused by it.'

He considered me. He was half-turned from the hearth, in his hand a stick which he had been using to adjust the pieces of wood on the fire. 'Would you write something for me?'

Although he made the request in a relaxed, even in an offhand way, and without evident anxiety, I sensed that my answer was of great importance to him. 'I would be very happy to try,' I said. 'What is it you want me to write?'

He looked about my room, as if he looked for something, then he turned back to the fire, which was well alight by now and burning brightly. He poked at it with the stick nevertheless. 'I would write it myself,' he said, a flicker of annoyance in the way he poked at the fire, 'but I can't do it. I write reports and am often the advocate for my people but I have not been able to write this story. I don't know why that is. I can tell it, but I can't write it.' He twisted around and looked at me. 'Why is that, do you think?'

I was about to respond with some conjecture or other when he went on, not waiting to hear what I might have to say.

'I've tried. Often. But I can never get it down on paper the way I have it in my head. I use the same words as when I tell it to myself but something is lost. It used to anger me. It still puzzles me. If I can tell the story, why can't I write it?' Once again he did not wait for me to respond but turned back to the brick hearth in front of him and set about rearranging the pieces of burning wood with his stick, as if he sought an ideal arrangement for them and would not be satisfied until he had found it. 'When Vita went to the university,' he said, pausing to struggle with a flaming log, 'I thought she would write the story for me one day. But she was soon busy with her own concerns and I saw that she was never going to find the time for it.' He turned from the fire again and looked at me. The fire might have been his principal concern and my presence little more than an adjunct to his purpose. 'I'm the only one left who knows the truth of what happened. If it's not written down the truth of it will be lost when I die. It was told to me by my grandfather. It was his own father, my great-grandfather, who did these things and told him of them. No one else is left alive today who knows the truth of it but me.' He waited, looking at me, and eventually he smiled slowly at something he saw in my features. 'I think of it all the time.' He shrugged, as if apologising for his seriousness. 'My fear is that I will die suddenly and it will be lost. That's what I fear, Max. Not to die, I don't fear that any more than you do. What I fear is to lose the truth of this thing.' He waited again, as if he expected me to say something.

'I will do my best,' I said. 'But I may not be the writer you imagine me to be.'

He sat looking into the flames, touching the stick to the burning wood until it glowed. He held the stick up and blew on the end of it until it took fire. 'My father was a dangerous man,' he said, narrowing his eyes at the small flame he held before his face. He waved the burning stick at me, as if he wrote a word in smoke with it. 'This is not it,' he said. His voice grew in confidence by the minute, and as he spoke he acquired an air of greater authority. 'You should know something about my life. How I came to have the truth of this thing, or you will not be able to write it.' He turned to me and I saw my reflection in the lenses of his spectacles—there I was for an instant, a prim white midget propped in bed against an even whiter ground of sheets and pillows. I was scarcely more substantial than a tiny ghost. He waited, the stick poised in his hand—a smoking baton. 'Before my father's and grandfather's time, we were leaders among our people because of our size and our courage. I'm not boasting. That's the way it was for us. It was our tradition that we feared no one but freely offered help to our neighbours when they needed it. Distant peoples turned to us and asked for our help. If their claim was just, they knew we would not refuse them. That is what we were known for, as other people are known for other skills. It was no secret but was our tradition and we were respected for it far beyond the borders of our own country. And, of course, we were also feared for it. Our reputation lodged in the minds of evil people and they thought twice before lording it over their neighbours.' He watched the end of the stick burning in the fire. I watched the stick burn with him. When the stick was well alight and the flames began licking towards his hand he set it on the fire and sat back. The air in the room was grey with wood smoke. It touched the back of my throat, just as it had when I sat of an evening with my uncle over our meal in his kitchen—the smell of wood smoke and the unresolved enigmas of my childhood.

'My father was a big man,' Dougald said. 'He had three sons. We all grew into big men. The old days were gone but we still carried the size that had been bred in us. When we were boys, my father worked on the railways in a maintenance gang out west and was away from our home for long periods. When he came home he stayed drunk for several days, and while he was drunk he beat me with the fury that was in him. There was a spirit in my father that enraged him and which he could not control or understand, and when he drank this spirit got the better of him. I believe it was the loss of the old ways, and of the respect we once enjoyed, that enraged him, though I don't think he ever understood this himself. I was his eldest son and he beat me in particular before all the others. He drank overproof rum straight from the bottle. Alone and at home, sitting at the kitchen table, brooding and silent for hours. The others left the house and went to our aunty's place, or sometimes they hid from him out in the scrub at the edge of town. But I sat by the back door and watched him.

'At first, when he had only had one or two drinks and was still sober, he told me stories of the fettlers' camps where he lived alongside the line out in the flat country towards Longreach, and how they called to the passengers on the passing trains to throw them the newspapers and begged tobacco and drink from them. After a few drinks he grew quiet and his mood darkened. And out of this dark silence he began to curse his fellow workers, or to curse some foreman or boss who came into his mind. At last he noticed me sitting in the doorway watching him and he called me to him. I stood in front of him and for a long time we were both silent, looking at each other. I knew then it had begun. Some force in me, superior to my will, made it impossible for me to speak or to run away. I always believed that if I had spoken to him, he would have broken from his drunken trance and would have forgotten to beat me. But I could not break my silence any more than he could break his trance. I still do not understand what power it was that robbed me of my voice, but only that it was a force greater than my own will.

'I stood no more than an arm's length from him. Always in the same attitude, my hands held behind my back, my thumbs hooked over the belt of my shorts, my feet bare. And always I was without a shirt. Our eyes were on the same level. His eyes were like deep wells and I looked into them and could never see all the way to the bottom but found my own gaze lost in their depths, as if I looked into his soul and into my own soul, and saw only our solitude. I loved my father and I can smell him now that I have begun to speak of him. He had a peculiar smell that was him and no one else. Without warning he hit me with the back of his hand. His blow struck my cheek and knocked me to one side. I did not step back or cry out, but righted myself and stood as before, looking into the solitude of his gaze. Then came the second blow. He beat me in silence. One blow following another. I did not cry out and there was no fear in me, nor do I have any memory of the pain. When the blood was flowing freely down my face and over my bare chest, and his hand was red with it, and he had lost control of what he did, and had begun to cry out as he struck me, my mother came into the house and she took me by the arm and led me away and bathed my injuries. If she had not done this my father would have beaten me until he killed me. And I would have stood and not run away. To me that is all a mystery now. After my mother had taken me away from him my father roared and bellowed like a bull that is tormented by a pack of dogs, and my mother and I looked at each other and we knew it was over.

'That night he came to my bedroom and took me in his arms and wept. And I forgave him. I loved him. He was my father and I wept with him for the loss we had sustained. My sisters and brothers lived in great fear of him, but I did not fear him. He never succeeded in making me afraid of him. He asked me often, *Why don't*

you run away from me and hide like the others? I had no
answer for him. I believe the spirit of violence in him was
provoked more than anything by my lack of fear, by what
he took to be my stubbornness and my resistance to him.
But still I never found a way within myself to show him
the fear that might have satisfied him. Even as a small
child, when he beat me I saw in the emptiness of his gaze
that he was punishing something within himself that he
hated and did not understand and could not reach, and
I did not think it was my father who beat me but some
other, a demon.

'Until the day he died, I saw in my father's eyes a
bewilderment and a despair so deep it had no bottom to
it and it made my heart ache to see it and I thought how
it might have been otherwise with him and me if he had
not been cursed in this way. And I knew he had always
been a lost man. It is as if he had searched in vain for
an answer to the riddle that cursed him from the day of
his birth. He asked himself, *What is it I am supposed to
do?* And he had no answer. I shall never forget my father
holding me to him and sobbing and asking in a voice
filled with anguish, *Why do I beat the boy I love the most?*
As if he expected God, or some other power greater than
himself, to answer him, but heard only the silence, which

he had learned to take as contempt for his kind. I wept with him for his torment, and I knew in my heart that he beat me because he knew that only I could withstand the beating. He might have killed one of the others in his rages and my mother might not have been able to prevent it. I stood between him and the terrible possibility that he might murder one of his children. And our knowledge of this stood between us and it was our bond.'

Dougald stopped speaking and he held his hands out in front of him and looked at his open palms. He was moved by the story he told me. 'I have never told anyone this,' he said. His hands were the misshapen hands of a workman. He held his large palms open before him as if they were an open book from which he read his memory. At last he shook his head and put his palms together, then turned and looked across at me and he smiled that soft and yielding smile he had, which was both an invitation and an acknowledgment of trust, and which I found bewitching. But it was also a sad smile, in which there was a kind of apology, or an appeal, and something of shame for what he was about to say. 'There are no stories I can tell in praise of my father,' he said then.

I was greatly moved by this confession and wished to speak, for what he said touched me and my own relations with my father very deeply, but he continued without a pause, and seemed not to wish to hear from me, his attention inward still.

'I believe my father's remorse for the pain he caused, and for the evil things he did, was genuine. I can say that for him.' He shrugged. 'Sometimes I wonder what I really knew of him. Most of his life was spent away from us. It was my mother who made a family of us.' With this mention of his mother Dougald sat more upright and he lifted his arms and stretched, as if he freed his muscles from his father's violent tyranny. 'My mother,' he said with feeling. 'She was an educated white woman from the city. She feared my father, but she also loved him and often took his part, even against his own people. My mother remained loyal to my father until the end. I was no longer at home in those days but was out there fencing with my grandfather. Against everybody's advice my mother cared for my father in his final years when he was infirm and at his most vulnerable. That was a time when many of his own people who had once feared him turned on him and taunted him. I never knew my mother to complain about my father, nor would she ever hear a word said against him. I believe she sensed something of the deeper causes of his rage as I did, and because of this she found the courage in herself not to judge him. She had married him and had taken her vows in the church and, although she never afterwards spoke to a priest that I remember, she held true to her vows until the end. In her own way she loved him. On the day we buried him, when we were all gathered in the kitchen of the old place, she told us, *Remember, all of you, this man was your father.*

'His own father, my grandfather, was a very different man. He was known as Gnapun. Although I never heard him claim it, I believe he had received from the Old People the benefits of the passage to manhood when he was a boy. Unlike my father, my grandfather was a man who knew himself. He was sober and hard working and was well liked and respected in his own country, both by the whites and the blacks. When I was nine, and had been in the hospital with the injuries my father had given me, my grandfather heard of it and he came to our house and took me away. Despite my father's drunkenness and his violence, my grandfather showed him respect. I saw how those two, father and son, shared a bond that nothing would ever break. I felt the power of it between them and have not forgotten it. It made me understand that there was something strong in our family that went beyond each of us, and that this thing had never broken despite my father's fierceness, but had held fast under the severest test. Strange as it must sound to you, this made me proud to be who I was, which was not something I had ever found easy.

'My grandfather took me to live with him in his caravan to the south of our town, in the country of his Old People over there in the valleys that lead up into the Expedition Range. There were few of his people living there at that time but he got me a place in the school in town because of the respect in which he was held there. In my first year I was required to fight the white boys in order to keep my place, but I was a good fighter and had no fear of them, and in time we made our peace and friendships grew up between us that have remained strong to this day. I still have many friends down that way, white and black, men and women. That was how it was when I was a boy. After we fought we became friends. Now things have greatly changed and we live in a time in which enmities endure. My grandfather was a contract fencer and when I was fourteen I left the school and went to live with him in his camp, and he trained me in the skills of fencing, which was the trade I followed most of my life until I took on being a cultural adviser and an advocate for our people up this way. Such things as cultural advice did not exist back then. No doubt my grandfather was already an old man in those days, but he did not seem old to me. He was youthful and strong and, despite living alone for many years since the death of my grandmother, he had kept his sense of humour and his love of life and nothing would have amused him more than to see me being who I am today and giving out so-called cultural advice to the whitefellas. Also there was an eagerness in my grandfather to work that is usually found only in young men. I loved him greatly and believed he had always been as he was then and that he would live forever and never change but would endure as Gnapun, my grandfather. He was gentle and kind and did not permit me to be in awe of him, but often asked me for my opinion and shared his thoughts with me, as if he believed me to be his equal.'

Dougald fell silent and sat looking at the creaking embers of the fire. I think he had forgotten I was there. But then he recollected himself and he turned to me and stood up and said, 'We'll talk some more tomorrow night, old mate. It's late. You need your rest. Once I start, I'm as bad as Vita.' He stood a moment, hesitating, as if he would say more, then he leaned and picked up the empty wood box from beside the hearth. At the door he paused.

'Vita asked me where you'd buried her goat. I told her you'd buried her high on the bank where the floods won't reach her.' He turned to leave. 'I'll bury the old nanny tomorrow. Goodnight, old mate.' He turned and went out and closed my door behind him.

As I lay there in my bed in the silence after he had gone, listening to the moaning of the wind in the scrubs and the creaking of the embers of my fire, his voice was still sounding in my ears. I wondered if Vita had told him that our inability to memorialise the deeds of our fathers was an affliction he and I possessed in common.

14

The writer

Sitting by the fire in my bedroom one evening soon after this, Dougald told me the story of his great-grandfather, the warrior Gnapun. It took him little more than an hour to tell me the story, but it took me ten long nights of arduous labour to produce a version of it I was prepared to let him read. *Told* the story to me? Well no, he placed his story in my care, and might have been giving his only child into my trust. It was a responsibility for which I felt myself to be unfitted. 'I am not Henry James,' I said to him when he finished the story that night and asked me if I would write it for him. 'I am only a journeyman historian. I think you need a poet for this.' I reminded him of Nietzsche's conviction that the work of the historian is devoid of the creative spark. But he would hear none of this and impatiently dismissed my objections. 'You're not that fella. You can do it, old mate,' he said. I was certain he did not truly appreciate the difficulties of the task he had set for me. I did not appreciate the true extent of them myself.

After Dougald left me that night, when the fire in my grate had burned down to a few embers and the silence was punctuated by the call of a mopoke deep in the great scrubs, I took up my journal and began at once the labour of composition. I did not want to fail him and knew myself to be unprepared for the task. I hoped to catch his tone and so wrote while his presence in my room and the sound of his voice were still fresh in my mind. His manner had been gentle and intimate, as if he placed the precious hoard of his story in my safekeeping, his presence in the quiet room lending to the images from his great-grandfather's time something I not so much heard in his words as observed in him—in the small gestures of his hands, in the firelight seeking the folds and crevices of his dark expressive features, his eyes indeed *looking* his great-grandfather's country into the room with us as he spoke.

I was kept in bed still with my badly twisted ankle and when he brought in my breakfast the following morning I did not tell him I had begun the work. I was too shy and too uncertain of what I did. I laboured at the composition secretly and at night. His manner of telling the story had suggested to me the expansiveness of an epic. *Egil's Saga* it might have been, the way he told of the exploits of his great-grandfather. But how to capture such effects and give them permanence on the page? As I began my work that first night it was with a feeling of regret that the writing of a story cannot be as its telling is, and even while I strove to put down only Dougald's words, and to rigorously avoid a distortion of his story with my own additions, I was conscious that the spirit of his story had been contained as much in the shapely vessel of his telling as it had in the sequence of its narrative.

Indeed, I soon found it was not possible to keep myself entirely out of it and, as I began to live more deeply within the events over the following nights, the spirit of Dougald's story and the spirit of my own story merged in my imagination and became one—until I *was* Gnapun the warrior and *he* was me. It was no longer the exploits of Dougald's great-grandfather that I wrote of, but became the deeds of an imaginary and heroic self—

none other than that same brave good man whom I had longed to become when I was a boy peering anxiously through the hole in the wall of my bedroom! And it was of that same great battle that I wrote now; that old struggle within us all to be good and just and to do no evil, a struggle which finds its final resolution in our death. It was only when I at last conceived the story in these terms that were intimate to myself that I was able to compose a version of it that at all pleased me. The question of whether it would please Dougald, however, or dismay him, remained undecided and was a source of great anxiety to me. In making his story my own, I feared I may have betrayed him, as a poor translation betrays the work that inspires it. Or had I—this faint hope in my heart—by giving his story a voice that was intimate to my own voice, found the only means by which I might offer him, in a written version of his story, the illusion of the intimacy of his own interior voice? It was a conundrum and I did not attempt to resolve it. I read over my story many times but could not answer this question to my satisfaction. When I finally handed it to him it was with my doubts and worst fears intact. His reading would have to give me my answer. Nothing else could. I titled his story 'Massacre'. It was a true and apt title for his story, of this

I have no doubt. But it was—and I alone knew this—also a title closer to my own history of failure than any other title or subject that I might have chosen to speak of from my own experience. When I finished it, I felt I had at last written my own book of massacre.

15

Massacre

To choose the moment of his own death. There was a nobility in that. The vision had been with him even in childhood and had persisted. Towards dawn in the escarpment high above the valley a disc of silver slid between the trees, touching the rocks with its aluminium light. When the cold light reached him he stirred in his sleep. A few moments later he sat up and tossed aside his cloak and rose from beside the ashes of his fire. Leaving his possessions in his sleeping place within the overhang of the cliff, he began the long descent by the light of the moon to the camp of the messengers. He carried only his favourite spears and travelled alone. An hour later the sun struck the peak behind him, but he did not turn to look back at the gilded mountain. He knew who the messengers were. He had known long before they arrived that they would come into his country and wish to speak with him of their troubles. He reached the wide meadows at the base of the valley and walked without haste between the black trunks of the great ironbark trees, the ground mist breaking before him, as if he breasted a pale tide in his nakedness, his body shining with the vigour that was in him, his limbs strong and well-proportioned, his long stride assured and full of purpose. He met no one, and as he advanced through his country he did not look about him, for he knew what lay to his left and to his right, but kept his eyes always to the front, his gaze touching the ground where he would tread. The sun was well up when he paused at the river to drink.

He caught a drift of the perfumed smoke from their fire among the leafy river gums before he saw them. They were camped on the sandy spit beside the long waterhole where he and his people had left for them the sign of welcome. There were four of them. He stood on the bank above them, and they quietly rose and looked at him, but did not utter a single word. He stood a while, neither moving nor greeting them, but permitting the morning stillness to settle around him after the disturbance of his arrival; giving these supplicants occasion to consider their position, allowing them a little time in which to wonder if he may not have come to them alone after all, but had his warriors concealed nearby. Standing above them on the high bank of the river he saw, in the nervous glances they exchanged with each other, how they travelled in their uncertainty to the scene of their own imminent destruction and looked with longing to where their weapons were concealed. He saw too how filled with anxiety the long night had been for them, for they had burned a great deal of wood during the hours of darkness, and had surely risen with the moon, having already breakfasted on several roasted ducks, the abundant remains of which were scattered around their sleeping places.

He called a low greeting to them then and, laying aside his spears on the grass, he went down among them. They were moved by his trust and returned his greeting eagerly, all speaking at once and complimenting him on the waterhole and the plentiful fish and duck, and thanking him for his generosity in providing such a campsite. Soon they had begun to relax and to smile and even to make a few jokes, the tallest of them saying, with cheeky bravado, 'Well, boys, what say we come and live here and fetch our families with us?' The others looked uncertainly at Gnapun when their lanky companion said this, and only laughed when they saw that Gnapun himself was amused.

Their laughter broke the tension of the morning and they tossed more wood on their fire and at once gained greatly in confidence. They sat together, watching the new wood take fire and begin to blaze noisily. And soon the tall man who had made the risky joke began to speak with animation of the trouble that had caused them to leave their families and had brought them three days through the empty scrubs of the miserable brigalow country from their own valley to speak with him. As he spoke of their troubles this man became increasingly agitated, gesturing wildly with his long skinny arms, and shouting unnecessarily loudly into the morning, his eyes shining like the eyes of a madman, until one of his companions was moved to lay a hand on his thigh and to advise him softly, 'It is better if we are calm, or our friend will not understand the gravity of our situation.' The tall man apologised and calmed down for a minute or two, but soon grew agitated again and started shouting and flinging his arms about just as before, which made his account difficult to follow in its detail.

Gnapun said nothing but observed the man's three companions—who evidently left the talking to their excitable friend because it was not possible for anyone to silence such a man for long. But his shouting and his wild jerky movements were a kind of silence in themselves, for they left the others at liberty to reveal their feelings in the private expressions that remained unguarded on their troubled features. Watching them, Gnapun saw that their fear was real, and that there was a deep panic in their hearts that they did not wish to let him see in case he judged them to be cowards and unworthy of his help. But he had seen this panic before in other men and it did not trouble him, for he knew the means by which frightened men can be made brave. At last he turned to the tall man and reached to lay his hand on the man's shoulder. Startled by the touch of Gnapun's hand, the man fell silent and stared at him, his eyes wide with astonishment and expectation. They waited anxiously for Gnapun to speak: It was clear he had made his decision.

He kept his hand on the tall man's shoulder and watched a pair of black swans that just then sailed fearlessly to the centre of the waterhole from the concealment of the rocks. Seeing the direction of his gaze the others turned and looked. 'It is time for us to leave this waterhole to the swans,' Gnapun said. 'I will return with you to your country through the brigalow and I will meet these strangers. When I have met them, I will decide if anything can be done about them.'

With great emotion the four men thanked him. The tall man wept, standing and turning away, shamed by his helpless tears. The others laughed at him gently and slapped each others' arms and apologised to Gnapun for him with their glances.

Gnapun said gravely, 'This is not the first time I have seen a brave man weep when he has reason to.' The tall man looked at him with gratitude for these words, and in that moment he became Gnapun's faithful follower and wished only to prove his courage to him when the time came for him to do so. Gnapun glanced to where he knew their weapons were concealed, which was his permission for them to retrieve them. 'We have a long way to go,' he said. 'We should leave at once.' A few minutes later they set off, carrying their long shafts at their sides and walking in single file behind the tall man, each careful to step into the footprints of the man he followed. Soon they had left their campsite far behind them in the possession of the black swans.

They walked all day down the narrow valley until it opened out onto the flat country where the haunted silence of the great scrubs awaited them, the thin trees tight-lipped here and not a word of comfort to be expected from them, but a shifting uncertainty in the flickering play of light and shade that might lead a traveller to lose his purpose and direction. They hurried on through the haunted scrubs without pausing until dusk each day, when they lit their small fires and rested until dawn. The messengers' spirits were strengthened on this return through the dismal scrubs by having the famous warrior Gnapun as their companion, the hope in their hearts now that when he saw how badly things stood for them with the strangers he would become their champion and would help them. Their situation, they knew, was hopeless otherwise.

* * *

Gnapun's people feared the visionary seizures that possessed him before a battle, and he had been required by custom since his early youth to sleep alone in order to remove from them the dangerous contagion of his powers. That night, in the desolation of the waterless scrubs, while he lay sleeping beside the cold ashes of his poor fire—the messengers were camped together some way from him—Gnapun was visited by a vision of such power it woke him with a start as if a woman slapped his face. He sat up, chilled and sweating, a deep pain gathering around his heart. There was no moon yet and he crouched beside the ashes of his fire in the blackness of the strange night, the deathly pain a tight band around his chest, like grief. It was surely death who had breathed on him while he slept. In the vision that haunted his waking eye he knew himself to be his own chief victim and understood that while he slept he had been magically inserted into the person of the leader of the band of strangers who had invaded the country of the messengers. In his vision he bore witness within himself to the slow death of this mortally wounded man, who was himself and was not-himself, a white man and a stranger to him, yet intimate and familiar, dear to him in ways he only knew but did not understand.

He saw through the dying man's eyes as he lay on his side in the noonday sun. Through the crisscross of the trellis in the vegetable garden, beyond the patch of bare ground where he was lying like a piece of meat baking on the stones, he could see his wife. She was no longer young but was a handsome woman all the same. She was his faithful life's companion and had shared his dreams and trials with him for thirty years or more. He loved her as he loved no other and knew no life without her by his side. He had lived in order to please her and his God. As she leaned forward, listening now, her dark hair falling across her face, he recalled the moment he had submitted willingly to her enchantment. Her hair shone now in the sunlight as it had then, falling lightly against the collar of her flowered dress. On her head the pale straw hat with the ribbon that lifted and was held by the breeze for an instant, then was released to trail over the flowers of her dress, like an indrawn breath that is held in expectation, then is slowly exhaled. She was standing very still, as if she had been alerted by a sound and was listening, her arms hanging emptily at her sides.

She was looking away from him towards the hills, which were a smoky blue and just the colour of the ribbon in her hat.

He made to raise himself then, but cried out with the thrust of pain in his side where the spear had entered him and opened his liver, its fierce quartz point lodged deep in the marrow of his pelvis. The pain was great and he closed his eyes and sobbed, his body trembling, the sweat coming out of him like grease from the flesh of a swan on the coals. When the pain subsided a little and he opened his eyes again his wife was no longer there. He heard her scream then. It was a howl sucked from her lungs by the agony of her moment. The terrible sound flew away into the emptiness of the morning, birds rising from the trees and shrieking with it, the air startled and the branches trembling. He felt his wife's howl in his chest and the horror of his helplessness in her moment of utmost need. To know he could do nothing for her. He was unable even to brush at the flies that swarmed over his face, probing for the moisture in the corners of his eyes, his nostrils and his parted lips, as if he was theirs and had been provided to them by their unearthly god. He murmured a prayer to his own God, his Saviour, the Lord Jesus Christ, or perhaps it was directly to his God that he addressed himself at this last: O Lord forgive them!

The meat ants had found him and had begun to enter him. He would have twisted around and inspected the wound in his side, and might even have attempted to draw the spear, but the pain was so exquisite his body would not obey the command of his will and he was not able to stir. After her scream the stricken day was filled with the chorus of the cicadas. He could see his pocket Bible, given him by his father more than fifty years ago on his tenth birthday, and never away from him since that day of blessed memory. It was lying in the dust two yards in front of him where it had flown from his hand, like a sudden black bird released when the heavy blow of the spear felled him. Lying beside his Bible were his broken spectacles, their lenses blindly reflecting the sky—reading eternity. The sacred book had fallen open and the light airs riffled its fine pages, as if an invisible hand searched the text for a suitable passage with which to memorialise the moment.

Above the hills white clouds bloomed. He imagined the clouds to be bed sheets tossed by an exuberant housewife. Perhaps his wife had been looking at the clouds and this was her thought that had entered his mind. He had often known himself to be one with her. They were companions of the flesh as well as of the spirit. This the secret truth of their love, the bond that united them and which had never been spoken of, but had been enacted. Another long drawn-out howl ended in a choking sob. He waited in the shrieking silence of the cicada chorus, his heart hammering, the sweat running from his pores, knowing the moment of her death now . . . But what was it to wait in this way after the death of the beloved? Now that the world was no longer his, for what did he wait? He was thinking of their two eldest sons, seeing the mob of sheep moving easily ahead of their horses, a fine dust in the air, the boys travelling the mob through the great scrubs far to the south. The boys would be finding abundant feed along the way, for it had been a good year for rain and everyone was happy and filled with optimism by this, and the sheep would not lose their fine condition.

It was true, he had been careful to choose his moment and had been commended, and even envied, for it. His move to the north had been soundly based, cautious and well planned, a certain boldness of purpose made explicit to the admiring crowd of onlookers at the moment of their departure for these distant pastures to the north. There had been a natural expectation of establishing themselves here successfully. Theirs had been the most numerous, well-armed and best-equipped party ever to enter this region. He was proud to have been the leader of such a community of Christian men, women and children. To have done this was to have done more than most men aspired to do. And it was such a place of beauty and abundance. A place blessed by God. It had been a cause of great rejoicing among them when, on drawing up here, they found a plentiful supply of perfectly mitred stones lying about on the ground waiting for their skilled hands to build the walls with. This blessed place had needed only their presence to complete it and they were confirmed in their belief. They had dismounted and offered thanks. He had known an inevitability in removing his family and his flocks to this place, for the voice of God's messenger had come to him in the night and commanded him to go forth into the wilderness with his family and his flocks. It had been a venture determined by a higher motive than mere advancement of fortune. In coming here he had known himself to be the instrument of God's plan. It is Providence that has set me here, not the greed of country that drives ordinary men into the bountiful wilderness with their flocks. This he knew in his heart. His purpose was a vision of love.

And he was modest in his love of his stewardship of this land. It is as if we have come home, he said to his wife that first night as they lay together under the stars. He was astonished to know a certainty in himself that the land had once been the home of his own true ancestors and was familiar to his blood. He even loved, with a kind of sad and helpless amusement of feeling, the little trellis that John made from wattles that first day. And loved too, in this same gentle and indulgent way, the vegetable garden his wife and the girls tended with the help of the women of these people. But, before anything, he loved these people themselves, and knew himself charged by God to bring them into the light of His redemption. Against the cautioning of his neighbours that they were not to be trusted as were the natives of the south from where he had come, he welcomed them into his home with respect and offered them the gift of the Gospels. He spoke with them of the great mystery of the love of Jesus Christ, Lord and Saviour, redeemer of mankind. Death shall have no dominion. This blessed place. And they, these naked and benighted children of the wilderness, smiled into his eyes and accepted his gifts and took the hand of welcome he extended to them, holding his fingers softly in their own, entering his home at his wife's modest entreaty, shy, trusting, curious and ready to believe. He was possessed by the passionate justice and the beauty of his vision of a Christian society in which black and white were to live in equal fellowship and not as master and slave. He knew himself to be no ordinary man, and that his new neighbours called him a fool, but he did not feel the passing shadow of imperial arrogance in his soul as they did. We have so much to learn from them, and they from us, he told his wife, her hand warm in his. And the sons and daughters of our mingling shall people a new Eden. It was his dream. It was her dream. Their shared vision of establishing Paradise on earth. He invited these people to sit at his feet while he read to them from the sacred Book: In the beginning God created the heaven and the earth. And he saw how their eyes shone to hear the words. It is the book of God's great plan, he told them, and promised to teach them the secret art so that they might read it for themselves . . .

From beyond the vegetable garden, at the place where he saw his wife a moment ago—if it were only a moment ago, for he was no longer clear about the lapse of time since the blow of the spear felled him—where she stood then, now a naked young man stands. The young man is looking at him, his skin shining in the sunlight as if he is cast in polished bronze. He is tall and beautiful and is perhaps no more than twenty years of age. He knows him. He is the young man who approached them on the track when they were riding out inspecting the country and with whom they exchanged a degree of confidence, his manner intelligent and quick, evidently understanding at once the benefits and the dangers to his people of the arrival of such a strong party as theirs. The unexpected assurance with which the young man addressed them in his own language, as if he believed himself to reside at the linguistic centre of the world, a place to which all men must aspire, and that they would understand him. It was with a smile that he told them his name, as if he believed they would have cause to remember it, or perhaps believed they already knew it. 'Gnapun,' the young man murmured in his soft voice, touching himself lightly on the breast with the tips of his fingers and smiling. It was as if he said to them, I am the black prince of this domain. He smiles now, perhaps from his memory of their meeting, then he turns and walks away, not looking back nor hurrying his pace. He is carrying something that swings heavily from his right hand, the set of his shoulders compensating for the weight of his burden, and he calls to his companions, who are farther off, gathered within the shade of the great dark tree that first attracted them to this spot as they approached . . .

Could it really have been a trellis through which he saw the figure of his wife? And then the figure of the young man? Or was it in the delirium of his agony a deceiving lattice of cast shadows from the slim stand of gum trees? Could it really have been a vegetable garden? Had they been here long enough to have established such a garden? Had they been here years? Decades? A lifetime? Or only days? Hours even? He no longer knows. Certainty has slipped from his mind and the shattered structures of his delusions draw him deeper. It is growing dark. The white pages of the book lying out there in the sun are a distant star now, the flickering pages signalling a message to him that he will never understand. If only he could have one last moment of lucidity . . . Or was it simply that his wife turned to him and remarked when they drew up here, There is the perfect place for a vegetable garden, and at her words of hope he saw a well-ordered garden such as the one she had cultivated at Mount Erin? A period of nineteen days is in his mind. Or is it only sixteen? But that cannot be right. There are nineteen of them all told in the party, this he is certain of.

The smell of burning is growing stronger and he is finding it difficult to breathe. Behind him he is aware of the conflagration, the house is burning, roaring, cracking and splitting, exploding into the shrieking air. They are all dead. They are all dead. His wife is dead, his daughters. All of them lie in their blood. Butchered and destroyed utterly. Or is it God who has died? He who drew them here only to abandon them? With his last breath he cries out the question that he has known men of his kind to cry out at their faithless end for thousands of years: My God, my God, why have you forsaken us? He enters the darkness alone.

There is no companion at his side. No God waits to receive him.

When the moon rises he steps silently across to where they sleep and wakes the messengers. They leave the night camp and make their way cautiously through the listening scrub. As he walks behind the tall messenger all that day and the following day Gnapun rehearses the scenes of his vision, his hand tightening involuntarily on the long shaft at the moment of driving the point into the leader's side. He is hungry and they have drunk no water now for two days and there has arisen in his thoughts this nagging, disgruntled suspicion that such visions as these do not always see events with certainty, but that jealous demons sometimes mislead men who dare to exercise the power of foresight. His own father also possessed this ability to dream himself his own victim before the death blow was given. But there is no place for such knowledge with the rest of his people, so he lives a life of privileged isolation, looked up to and feared, as princes always are. That he must keep such knowledge to himself makes him lonely and he longs to take a wife and to have her companionship at his fire as other men do, and one day to see his own children. As he walks hour after hour behind the tall messenger his hunger and his thirst make him wish to be an ordinary man welcomed among his people.

So they travel together for three days to the country of the messengers and there he recognises the place of his vision and knows it already, even to the detail of what he will see when the leader's dark-haired daughter takes his hand and leads him into their dwelling, observed and smiled upon by her mother and father. It is on the track that he meets the leader himself, the man he will kill when the moment comes for him to strike the blow. He is gratified to see the curiosity and the courage in the leader's steady gaze, and knows him at once to be a worthy adversary. He tells him his name. 'I am Gnapun,' he says, touching himself on the breast, and at this a smile is forced into their eyes. It is a smile of recognition and is filled with such lively intimations that they are both abashed by the unsettling intimacy of the contact. What deepness is this between them that they acknowledge? When the leader and his companions have ridden on a way, the leader lays a hand to the cantle of his saddle and he turns around and looks back. Gnapun is still watching him—the way death watches, dispassionately, for the moment when it will strike us down and see us come to our end. Seeing the leader turn in his saddle and look back at him, Gnapun lifts his hand and the leader returns his salute. They are brothers, there can be no doubt of it, and it is their brotherhood they acknowledge with their salute. Their intimation of familiarity. And in this moment they each know themselves to be men first and only the sons of their fathers by the accident of birth. One of them will surely slay the other. The unseen hand ceases to riffle the pages of the sacred Book, for it has found the passage it seeks: And now art thou cursed from the earth, which hath opened her mouth to receive thy brother's blood from thy hand . . . And so the fear in his heart. But what is there to fear if death is not to be feared? Gnapun asks himself. And he is remembering the night in the scrub when his heart cringed by the ashes of his fire and he knows there is something greater than death, something more terrible and more final, and he is aware that he has begun to wait for it and that it begins to possess him. He does not know what this thing is that he waits for, and his ignorance makes him uneasy and distracts him. He is not himself and speculates that perhaps some part of him does not belong to his people, but belongs only to himself, marking him for what is to happen. This sadness on his heart. Why must it always be like this?

When he and the messengers reach the camp of the strangers he is shocked to see the terrible evil that has been done there. No fiend, in all the great store of teachings, has ever been said to have done such a thing as this. He stands looking on at the nightmare before him, numb with disbelief. How is he to understand that one people can treat another in this way? The thought that enters his mind then is like a sharp splinter of poison and it makes him tremble: The strangers do not respect the reality of the messengers' people, but see them as beings who are less than human. What other explanation can there be for this horror? For the strangers have collected the stones of the sacred playgrounds of the messengers' Old People and have built walls from them. Gnapun turns to the tall messenger and he puts his hand on his arm and tears roll down his cheeks. They weep together helplessly. Even though there are old men among the messengers' people who know the position from which each stone has been taken, everyone knows that to restore the stones to their places would not restore them to their power. Having been taken from their places, Time has been brought to the stones and they are lost to the eternal present of reality. They were there, now they are not there. They have lost their position in the sacred Dreaming and their power to sustain the messengers' people can never be restored to them. Set once again in their old places, the stones would themselves only belong to the past and would be merely history, there to remind everyone of what had once been and has been lost. The messengers' people, Gnapun sees, as he stands there weeping beside the tall man, cannot survive this but have been made exiles in their own country. They have been rendered capable of suffering from their past, an evil previously unknown to them, and a punishment no people has ever had imposed upon it before this day. For as everyone knows, to suffer from one's past is a punishment without remedy. It is the end of belief. To sing, after this, would be a blasphemy. After this there can be no innocence. The Old People of the messengers have been banished and humiliated. How will anyone ever bring them back?

As he stands there in sorrow looking on at the scene of activity before him, the stone walls and bark cottages occupying the sacred site of the playgrounds of the Old People, the timber yards, the cows and pigs and sheep and the horses and the men and women, the terrific noise of everyone hurrying about their work, hammering and sawing and calling out to each other, the familiar trellis and the vegetable garden, he sees before him at last the thing that is greater than death and knows it for what it is. He is too stricken by grief for the people of the messengers to enter the camp of the strangers, and he turns away and walks alone into the forest and finds a place to lie down where he will not be seen. And there he stays and weeps, not eating or drinking, for three days and three nights. On the morning of the fourth day he rises and goes in search of the principal camp of the people of the messengers, and when he has eaten and his strength is restored, he speaks to the tall man of what must be done.

When the tall man calls the young men of his people to him they all come and not one stays away or finds an excuse to decline the invitation. They listen to Gnapun in silence and when he has told them his plan, they arm themselves and go with him readily to a waterhole in the thickest part of the forest not far from the camp of the strangers, each one of them considering it an honour to be a member of Gnapun's war party, and none fearing death so greatly that he does not welcome this opportunity to demonstrate his courage at the side of such a leader and to revenge his people. The tall man leaves nothing unsaid in praise of Gnapun, but is eloquent in his enthusiasm. 'Gnapun cannot die,' he shouts at the young men, waving his skinny arms over his head, so that their eyes follow his arms as if they follow little birds flitting about in the scrub. 'We may die but Gnapun will live forever, a hero in our hearts and in the hearts of our people,' he yells. 'And those who go to war with him will be remembered as heroes with him. This will be a war of vengeance, which we all know is the fiercest kind of war. It will be bloody and terrible and will help us for a little time to deal with this grief in our hearts. It is better to die as a warrior where the playgrounds of our Old People once stood, and to shed our blood there, than it is to live filled with hatred in shameful exile on our own country.'

When the tall man at last stops speaking, Gnapun cautions patience and, leaving his weapons with them at the waterhole, he goes alone into the camp of the strangers. Men and women are busy ploughing the ground and planting seeds, and yet others are baking bread and milking cows. There is no end to the activity, and the country all around echoes to their shouting and laughter and to the bellowing of their milk cows and the bleating of their sheep. Gnapun goes among them, observing their enterprise, and seeing that it is their intention to change everything and to leave no sign of the old world. Already many of the great trees that have shaded the playgrounds for centuries have been cut down and sawn into lengths, the tender flesh of the timber gleaming palely in the sunlight where it lies, the sky open and blank.

He sees the woman with the dark hair watching him from the doorway of a hut and knows her to be the leader's wife. When she sees that he has noticed her she smiles and beckons to him. He walks across to her and stands before her, examining her. She reaches and touches him lightly on the arm with her hand. 'Gnapun,' she says and smiles. Her eyes are beautiful, her thoughts soft and dark and filled with curiosity and confidence. He touches her arm and then his own breast, asking her name, and she replies, 'Winifred.' They stand smiling at each other. She takes him by the hand and leads him inside the hut, where her two daughters are at work making cheese. The young women welcome him and show him their work with enthusiasm, the youngest taking his hand and directing him to touch the smooth handle of the churn. At the touch of the girl's hand the rage swells in his breast and he grips her fingers fiercely. She whimpers and shrinks away from him, and he smiles and releases her. Her mother goes to the girl and comforts her, looking at him with reproach, the air between them quivering. A shadow falls across Winifred's features and Gnapun turns to the door. The leader steps into the hut and greets him. Outside the hut Gnapun signs to the leader that he wishes to help, mimicking the actions of a man who is sawing timber nearby. The leader readily accepts Gnapun's offer of help and signs to him that if there are other strong young men like himself who are also willing to help, then Gnapun should bring them in and he will give them work. Gnapun observes the man and understands him with little effort. 'We are short of labourers,' the leader signs to him. 'Our ambitious building plans must be completed before the arrival of my two eldest sons and their numerous party, who are approaching through the southern scrubs with the flock.'

When Gnapun understands this, he knows that he cannot delay but must act swiftly, and he returns at once to the waterhole where the young men are waiting for him. He tells them he will take them into the camp of the strangers a few each day, so as not to alarm the strangers. 'You must make yourselves useful and act with friendliness and decorum at all times. When our entire war party has assembled in the camp of the strangers and they have grown accustomed to our presence and are at ease with us, then we shall destroy them. A night will come when I shall instruct you to arm yourselves with your favourite weapons. And the following morning you will come into the camp as usual, ready to work, and will each choose a stranger to slay and will stay close beside your chosen victim, your weapon concealed, which you all know well how to do. When we are assembled and I see that we are each of us in our place, I shall give the cry of the Wylah, the funereal black cockatoo, for you all know by now that this is the bird of my spirit and you will recognise my command in its cry above the clamour of these people. At the sound of the Wylah's cry you will deliver the death blow. If the strangers should be given a moment to sense our intention and to arm themselves, then our chance of success will be lost and we ourselves shall be the ones to lie on the old playgrounds at the end of the day in our own blood. And if by some mischance the battle is not going well and you see your friends and brothers dying around you, and you feel like running away, remember that Gnapun the warrior is with you and he will fight with you and will die in your country rather than run away to the safety of the scrub.' He does not disclose to them that the leader's two oldest sons are soon to arrive with their own men and a flock of sheep, for he does not want them to be distracted and to be forever looking over their shoulders during the battle.

Days go by and Gnapun takes the young men into the camp of the strangers in ones and twos and they willingly join in the work, bending their backs and shouting and laughing with the strangers, cheerfully sharing their meals with them and showing them the best places to catch fish in the river. It is not many days before the young men are skilled in the use of the axe and the crosscut saw and the iron wedges and the great heavy bars and have become well liked and respected by the strangers. One or two are much admired by the young women of the strangers and are inclined to respond to their smiles. Gnapun warns them not to be distracted in this way but to be alert for treachery. He points out one particular young man who is never without his weapon at his side. 'You have all seen him and know with what malice he regards us. He would give the order to shoot us all if his father were not to be a witness to it. This man is the leader's youngest son. He watches me closely and shows me great distrust no matter how I strive to beguile him with the innocence of my intentions. He is angry with his father for allowing us to join them and warns his father to be on his guard against us, telling him he should not have permitted so many strong and agile young men to come into the camp. His father lays his hand to his son's shoulder and, with a gentle smile, for he loves his son, he admonishes him, advising him to place his trust in the Lord and to treat us with respect and kindness, For that is the way of the Lord and it will profit us in the end. And he takes from the pocket of his black coat the book he always carries with him, just as his son always carries a weapon at his side, and he reads to his son from the Book. And his son listens in sullen silence to his father, who he respects and knows to be a worthy and a good man. And I John saw the holy city, new Jerusalem, coming down from God out of heaven, prepared as a bride adorned for her husband. This is your country he is talking about.

'And he reads much more than this, telling his son that the Book and not the gun will rule the new Jerusalem and that things will not turn out here as they have turned out in other places, where men of different creeds and races are forever in dispute with one another. This is the blessed country of our Lord, he says. He has prepared it for our coming and we are the first pioneers of His Providence. These people who are already here are the children of His country and from them we shall learn the ways of this land, which is their mother, and in return we shall give them the gift of the Gospels and the grace of our Lord Jesus Christ, who is the Saviour of all mankind, and they will make us welcome in their turn and this land shall be our mother also. And together, hand in hand, just as you see us working and laughing around you this very day, so the leader tells his son, we shall build the new Jerusalem. He that overcometh shall inherit all things; and I will be his God, and he shall be my son, so saith the Lord our God. Such is the promise to us of His great plan.

'The son listens to his father in silence, but in his heart he is not convinced that this plan of his father's is a good one. The son knows nothing of our plans, but he senses our intentions. He will not openly oppose his father, for he is a loyal son, but his father's words have no effect on the conviction in his heart. He senses our intentions because he is himself a young man just as we are and knows that if a powerful party of strangers were to come into his country and desecrate the sacred places of his land and take it from him and his brothers and sisters, then he and his brothers would not rest until they had taken their land back again and had revenged themselves. The leader's son understands something of this in his private thoughts,' Gnapun tells the assembled warriors, 'and he knows that young men, unlike old men and women and little children, will not stand meekly by when what is their own future is stolen from them and is destroyed, but will strike back with a tiger-like desire to annihilate. This young man cannot sleep at night, but lies awake in dread listening for our stealthy approach,' Gnapun tells them. The young men laugh at this picture of the leader's son waiting anxiously for them through the night, wakeful and alone, while they sleep peacefully by their fires. 'Our plan is to strike not in the night, however, when men are watchful and afraid, but in the bright morning, at that time of the day when a man's hopes are at their highest and his fears have been conquered, when death is furthest from his thoughts and there is a boldness in his beliefs that makes him see his own future with assurance in the day that remains to him to live.'

Gnapun has observed that the leader's son sometimes rides far into the scrubs to the south of the camp during the heat of the day, and he knows that he goes in search of a sign of the approach of his brothers and their party, hoping they will soon arrive to strengthen him against his father. Gnapun says nothing of this to the others but falls silent. Looking over the assembled warriors, he senses their eagerness for him to inspire them with the hot desire to kill the strangers, and so he addresses them with the words that come naturally into his heart at this moment, and which he is well satisfied will rouse their spirits to the fierce heat that is required if a man is to kill another human being, which he knows is not an easy thing to do.

'We are not going to leave a single one of them alive,' he cries out. And he shakes the long shaft of his favourite spear until it hums menacingly and fills the air by the waterhole with the sound of the great red hornet, promising the fiery sting of battle. 'We are not going to leave a single one of them alive,' he cries, 'down to the babies in their mothers' wombs—not even they must live. The whole people must be wiped out of existence, and none be left to think of them and shed a tear.' Gnapun turns to the tall messenger, who stands at his side, and he lays his hand on the messenger's shoulder and offers him the privilege of killing the leader's son, whose hand is never far from his gun. The tall messenger smiles and the young men look at him with respect and envy, eager to see on the day how he will perform this task. 'I shall deal with the leader myself,' Gnapun says. 'For he and

I are brothers and we know this is the way it is to be decided between us.'

The young men possess only a kind of vague poetic sense of what Gnapun might mean by this puzzling claim to be the brother of the leader of the strangers, but they do not ask him for any further explanation of his meaning, for they trust that if he wished them to have a fuller sense of his extraordinary claim at this time, he would give it to them without them needing to ask it from him. They are confident that one day the fullness of Gnapun's meaning will become clear to them. One day, if they survive the battle, long after these events, when they are old men and are walking alone through their own country thinking of nothing in particular, an understanding of Gnapun's meaning will suddenly blossom in their minds like the rare flower of the moon tree that blooms only once in a man's lifetime, and they will know what Gnapun meant when he stood before them and told them the leader of the strangers and he were brothers. Then they will pause in their walk and smile to see him once again as he was this day, a young warrior of great wisdom and strength who led them on that auspicious occasion without fear or hesitation. And for each of them, on the day of the blossoming of understanding, Gnapun the warrior will live again and they will know in their hearts the pride of having joined him in his resistance to the strangers; and they will remember their resistance was untarnished by unworthy motives but was a passion and a pure thing of the spirit. Then they will resume their solitary walk, old men nearing death themselves, accompanied by the thought that each man finds death in his own way and carries it within him in the manner of his character from his earliest days. Brothers, they will murmur aloud and will smile to think of the puzzlement they felt as young men.

'There are nineteen of them,' Gnapun says. 'If any of them live they will continue their leader's enterprise of the Book and will make of this their own story, and we shall not figure well in it but will be portrayed as the evildoers.'

When the day to arm themselves dawns, not a man among them can predict how that day will end for him, and as they leave the comfort of their fires and move out from their camp in the chill dawn, they consider Gnapun's words and they are in a mood either to kill or to be killed, whichever way events fall to them. Their skin glistens in the sun with the sweat of anticipation and unease and there is a tremor in their limbs that is like the tensioning within a deadly shaft that sings to itself with the power of the man who wields it before the instant of its release.

The moment they enter the camp of the strangers that morning, Gnapun feels the unease of the strangers. It is an unbidden rising of fear among the strangers that does not know itself or its cause, an unlooked for hesitation in the gaze of these people, a hesitation in the action of their hands and their limbs as they struggle to know the smooth and customary necessity of their daily work. He catches Winifred's uncertain glance and smiles, but she shakes her head and turns away and goes into the hut where her daughters work. Men involuntarily cast their eyes towards Gnapun, and one of the women cries out, then covers her mouth, shocked by the sound of her own alarm, for which there is no visible cause. There is a stillness of anticipation over the morning camp that makes the air tremble. Gnapun feels their bewildered terror running through them like a sickness and he knows that he and his warriors cannot waste a moment but must position themselves quickly and do the deed at once or be overwhelmed by the outbreak of fear, for a kind of panic is rising around him among these people and they are suffocating in its horror. They cannot draw breath freely and they stand and gape as if something grips them from within. A child's sudden wail of fear cuts the eerie silence and its mother cannot comfort it. The eyes of the strangers seek each other but there is no comfort or reassurance to be found. Each man and woman knows only the nameless terror in their own heart.

Gnapun sees the son of the leader of the strangers then. The young man is running towards them from the stockyards, where he has been supervising the work; he has drawn his revolver and it is in his hand. As he runs towards them he waves the revolver above his head, his mouth open. He is shouting a warning to his father, but his shout is held in the air by the urgency of his despair. He has seen that it is to happen and time has ceased for him and he knows he can do nothing but still he cries out and runs towards his father. The leader of the strangers stands close beside Gnapun on the bare patch of ground near the vegetable garden and he shields his eyes and looks anxiously towards his running son, fearing some dreadful accident at the yards.

Gnapun sees that every man is at his place and he stamps his foot, sudden and hard, on the claypan, making a drum-like sound that alerts the leader to his closeness. The leader begins to turn towards him, his son's warning taking hold in his astonished eyes, and he begins to tug the sacred Book from his side pocket and to make his turn, so that he can bring the Book to bear upon his black brother, his eyes meeting Gnapun's, his gaze beseeching, seeing the spear appear in Gnapun's hand as if from nowhere, and crying out in disbelief, 'No! Gnapun, my brother!' With the Book of God held out towards his brother he wards off the terrible knowledge that is rushing in upon him like the breaking of a great flood that will bear him away, and he clings like the drowning man he is to his broken dream of a new Jerusalem that has possessed him and has driven him, dispossessing him of his clear sight, his Christian vision in thrall to the gift he will bestow upon a benighted family of humankind. 'No, Gnapun!' he cries again, his fingers white against the black binding of his sacred Book, his other hand reaching to take hold of Gnapun's shoulder, his body off-balance and twisting in the ungainly turn.

Gnapun stays his hand, giving his brother time to search deep into his eyes and to take upon himself the fullness of his approaching death and to know it. Then he cries out with the wailing cry of the funereal Wylah and slips the fierce quartz blade into the cringing flesh of the leader and he bears on the shaft with all his weight and cries again with the cry of the great black bird of his spirit and the spirit of his fathers, lodging the hungry point deep in the bone of the leader's pelvis, so that the leader is flung violently to the ground, his scream unable to escape from his frozen lungs, the Book flying from his hand as he strikes the hard-packed earth on which the feet of the messengers' people have danced since before the beginning of time, his spectacles flying from his face and catching the morning sun in their flight—the eyes of a dead man. And still Gnapun bears on the groaning shaft. Then, with an abrupt flinging action of his hands, as if he is disgusted and wishes to rid himself of something distasteful, he relinquishes the shaft and steps away from the dying man. The man, who is himself.

'Keep my spear!' he shouts with a kind of wild, angry despair and he turns away. In the distance then he hears a single shot, but he does not look around to see how the others have fared. He turns his back on the leader and walks to the leader's house and enters by the door. In the darkness he stands while his eyes adjust, the cries and screams from outside rising now to a crescendo of human terror and dismay, the horror breaking upon the place as if it has been harboured there for centuries awaiting this moment of flowering. Gnapun sees the rifles in their rack and he gathers them and carries them outside and flings them to the ground. Still he does not look around him to see how the messengers' men have fared. He sees that life persists in the eyes of the leader, his gaze on the fluttering pages of the Book. He steps past the leader and picks up the Book and he places it with the rifles in a pile and makes fire. Without their Book they will have no plan.

Already he knows that the resistance he has begun this day will persist for the rest of his life and will never release him from its grip. This day he has become the man he was destined to become. He is himself, and he knows what it is to be alone—the cringing of his heart by the cold ashes of his fire in the depths of the scrub, the thing greater than death that he has struck down here but has not defeated. Since the banishment of the Old People the now has been lost and everything is subject to change. No man will ever again live within the moment but all people will be the victims of Time, this terrible thing that has been set free among them like a pestilence and will devour their souls. There is no one to whom he can tell his story and he will carry it silently in his heart like a beast that sleeps but will not die. As he watches the Book burn, the pages curling and flicking bright stars into the morning air, he thinks again that perhaps one day he will have a son to whom he will be able to pass on the burden of this story.

When the Book is ashes and the stocks of the rifles glow with the light of coals, he gets up and walks over to the leader and looks down at him. He sees that there is a thread of life in the man yet, a small light of broken dreams in his bewildered gaze, as if his gods have forgotten him and he already looks back at his shattered world in sorrow from a great distance, as if he looks back at the ruins of life from the infinite cavern of death, from the margins of that other world where he will never again meet his wife or his daughters or his sons, who are bringing the flock through the scrubs. The leader's hand moves against the hard-packed ground and Gnapun squats and takes his fingers gently in his own. Between them there is only the bewildering mystery of their brotherhood: *Thou has driven me out this day from the face of the earth; and from thy face shall I be hid; and I shall be a fugitive and a vagabond in the earth; and it shall come to pass, that everyone that findeth me shall slay me.* Gnapun caresses the leader's hand and lingers beside him. Then he lays the leader's hand on the desecrated ground of the messengers' Old People and stands. The leader is still now. His eyes have seen the last thing they will ever see. He is a dead man. He is too far away for even the kindest thought to reach him now. He is beyond consolation. The fires burn and their crackling is the only sound that breaks the silence of the morning.

Gnapun looks around him at last to see how the young warriors of the messengers' people have fared. The strangers lie where they have been felled, the men, the women and the little children. The ground is soaked with their blood and the air is filled with the hot stench of it and of their burning dwellings. Not one of the young men of the messengers' people lies among them. He sees the tall messenger watching him from beyond the garden but he does not approach him or offer him a sign. He turns away and begins the long walk home. Alone he walks for three days and nights through the unwelcoming scrubs and while he walks he wonders if any man will ever know the truth of his story, or if it will remain with him forever in the silence.

16

A made-up world

Cautiously I swung my legs over the side of the bed and with a gasp I stood up. My ankle was still tender but it held my weight shakily. Teetering unsteadily like an old drunk, I took my dressing-gown from the head of the bed and dragged it on over my pyjamas. I stood gathering my resolve, steadying myself with a hand to the bedhead, trembling and unshaved, my spectacles askew. I had not expected this wretchedness. Writing his story had been a secret and a nightly joy. I did not want to lose it. Alone with Gnapun and my journal I had forgotten this old age, this grief, this terrible decline and had lived again as a young man. No, I had not expected this euphoria to end with the end of the story, this sudden miserable fall into the banal realities of my poor existence. If it was a reward I looked for, then I had already received it. I gazed unhappily at my journal where it lay on the covers. I would have gone on with the story, but there was no more to be said. The story was finished. The bird had flown. My little journey into fiction was over. The surprise, more impressive in its way than my disappointment, was that what I had done was no longer mine. By finishing I had not gained something but had lost something, and I did not know how I might remedy the loss, or fill the gap it left in me, unless I were to write another story and to make my escape again by this means. But what story? I knew no stories. I picked up the journal and, clutching the cursed thing under my arm, hobbled out to the kitchen with it. No doubt Dougald would loathe it and Vita, when she read it, would be offended by my presumption.

Dougald was working at the table on his laptop as usual, surrounded by the disorder of his papers. He looked up as I lurched across the kitchen towards him. A pile of our unwashed clothes lay on the chair beside him. Some of the dirty clothes had fallen to the floor and the grey bitch had made her bed on them. She eyed me with distrust. The sink was also filled with dirty dishes. In my absence the household had slid back into the state of neglect and disorder in which I had found it. I was anxious and felt intensely irritated suddenly for no reason. I did not want to hand the story over to Dougald. My reluctance was partly that he would disapprove of it, but more than that, I felt I had made the story my own and that he would not understand it. I had *enacted* it on the page, word by word, night after night. I had *lived* it. I did not want to hand it back to him, just like that, as if it were merely his to receive and to thank me for, and there was to be an end of it. A job done. I resented both the possibility that he would calmly repossess it and that he would reject it. Neither would satisfy me. He did not look at me as I approached him but looked at the journal.

I set it on the table beside him. 'There,' I said. 'It's done.' It was not the generous spirit that I had expected between us at this moment. I had written it for him, after all, not for myself. Why was it so awkward for me now, and so fraught with this mean-spirited reluctance to part with it? He had cared for me since my foolishness that night without ever once complaining. Indeed he had probably saved my life at the stinking waterhole. And had I not wept while he held me in his arms? Under 'Massacre'

I had written, 'A true story by Dougald Gnapun'. For it
was not authorship in the usual proprietary sense that I
was laying claim to, but something more private than that,
something more intimate and intuitive. It was my *own*
secret that I wished to keep, a thing not to be disclosed or
shared with anyone. He looked up at me and I saw how he
doubted and hoped and was afraid and eager all at once
to know what I had done with his hero—I saw how he
had waited these last ten days and nights, as anxious all
that time as I was now. It seemed selfish and unfeeling
of him to me, the way he took the journal then into his
hands without a word. I hated him at that moment, with
the fierce hatred we reserve for our most deeply loved
intimates—as if a match is struck in our brains and flares
for an instant, leaving us ashamed and burned.

I stood beside him, calm enough it must have
seemed, but wanting to snatch the book out of his hands
and tell him, *You can't read it! It's not yours! It's mine!*
I felt certain he would not understand what I had written
as I understood it myself, and would perhaps even find it
offensive and a betrayal of the trust he had placed in me
to preserve the truth of his story. I said nothing, however,
but stood watching him read, compelled against my will
to read with him: *To choose the moment of his own death.*

There was a nobility in that . . . I could not bear it and murmured an excuse and hobbled out into the yard.

I stood on the concrete in the shade of the tree—it was a familiar haven, this place in the shade of the old tree; I had missed it. I was trembling and my heart was hammering with the confusion of emotions that had taken me so much by surprise. My two brown dogs watched me warily, as if they feared I might aim a sudden kick at them. 'Oh, it's all right,' I said. 'You needn't look at me like that. I just need a drink.' There was nothing to drink in Dougald's house. Early in our acquaintance, when one of his people had been drunk on the telephone, he had expressed such a fierce abhorrence for drink that I had understood him to fear it.

In the absence of the goat, the weeds and grasses had overgrown the yard. The place looked uncared for and abandoned. The grass swayed in the light airs, just the way my uncle's barley swayed when it was ripe and he and I stood admiring it and hoping we would get the reaper to it before a storm flattened it. And suddenly I could smell the sweet ripe barley fields of my childhood. I hobbled across to the shed and found a curved slasher among the hoard of tools there and I took it out into the yard and began to slash helplessly at the weeds. I had once known how to do this job efficiently. My uncle and I had reaped the headland swathe by hand before bringing the mechanical reaper into the field behind the horses. I bent from the waist and embraced an armful of the rank growth now and hacked at its base. Thistles prickled the palm of my hand and the blade was blunt. I kept at it.

My ankle was soon torturing me and my heart thudded so heavily I thought I must have a stroke or a heart attack. There was a perverse pleasure in defying the odds and keeping at it. *Go on, then, kill yourself and be done with it!* It was an attitude that amused my disdainful other self, who never did anything unreasonable or silly but preserved his dignity and his calm in the face of every extremity—he had not agreed with my original decision to kill myself and had mistrusted me ever since. But I was determined never to *be* him. I was sweating and threw off my dressing-gown and dropped it behind me. It amused me—the real, the helpless, stupid me, I mean—to think of Dougald coming out of the house when he finished reading the story and finding me sprawled on the ground on my back like the leader of the white strangers, the reaping hook tossed aside and glinting in the sunlight, his great-grandfather's spear sticking from my side. Was I the leader of the strangers? No. Never. I was only Gnapun

in my dreams; in reality I did not possess his great soul.
I knew that. But I was not the leader of the strangers . . . I
bent and gathered one armful of the prickly grasses after
another, gasping in the hot air, my mouth open, sweat
streaming down my face and back. My pyjama top was
soon wet with sweat and sticking to me. I tore it off and
threw it aside and worked on, naked to the waist. I was not
young. And I was not pretending to be young. But for this
brief season with the reaping hook in my hand it would
be *as if* I were young. My vision was blurred with sweat
and thousands of insects flicked around me, touching my
face and hands and sticking to my eyes. I kept working.
There was a joy in defying old age and pain . . .

The touch of Dougald's hand to my shoulder startled
me and I straightened and stared at him. He withdrew his
hand from my sweating skin and stood looking at me. My
chest heaved and the sweat cascaded down my face, the
reaping hook gripped in my hand as if it were the weapon
of a berserker. He held my journal and looked at me. The
air thickened in my throat and a terrible prickling dryness
threatened to choke me.

With a solemn and grave astonishment, he said, 'You
could have been there, Max.'

Joy and relief swept through me—a little tsunami it

was. And I wanted to repeat his words aloud—I *heard* them repeated aloud in my head. 'Oh, you like it then?' I said, my tone surprisingly conversational. A rush of well-being raced through my blood.

He stepped up to me and embraced me and held me strongly against his body, pinioning my arms to my sides. The point of the reaping hook was digging into my leg.

He released me and stepped away. 'Thank you,' he said.

I saw that he was greatly moved by what I had done for him. I wiped at the wet hairs sticking to my face and grinned at him foolishly. 'I'm glad you like it,' I said. 'So, it's okay then? That's good. I'm glad.'

'Oh yes, old mate,' he said, and he laid his open hand on the cover of my journal. 'It's all here.'

I said, 'Your approval means a great deal to me. I was afraid you might be offended by it.'

He smiled and reached out to put his hand on my shoulder and gave me a small shake, as if he forgave my foolishness and uncertainty. 'As soon as that ankle of yours is up to it, we'll take a drive down there to my country and pay the old Gnapun a visit.'

I said carefully, 'But of course he is no longer with us.'

'Gnapun's still with us, old mate.' He brandished my journal. 'His story's not over yet. We'll go up to that cave of his in the escarpment.' He was almost jubilant. Something real had happened. He had his wish. His precious story was preserved.

'Will you be able to find your way there?' I said. 'I mean, after all this time?'

He touched his chest with the tips of his fingers, just the way I had imagined Gnapun touching himself when he told the leader of the strangers his name. 'There's a map of my country in here.'

I was under the shower and was singing the Beatles' song, 'All You Need is Love'—or is it all *we* need? I am never sure—when the obvious struck me and I fell silent. It was the superior voice of my knowing other self, of course, and it rang like a bell in my head: *So you have identified yourself at last with the perpetrator of a massacre.* Was there a note of triumph in this claim? A gleeful delight at having caught me out? It was true. But it had not occurred to me. I would have liked to ignore it. Not once during those long nights struggling to bring Gnapun's story into being, those long nights of being him, the joy I had felt, the kindred intensity of my feelings, not once had I ever

249

experienced the remotest touch of guilt-by-association with the terrible crimes of that day. You would think I would have flinched. But I hadn't. By what knotted confusion of my unconscious reasoning, I wondered as I stood there under the cascading shower, had I considered myself to be in the clear with Gnapun? He and I were both members of this same murdering species. It was a puzzle to me how I could have composed his story with such a sense of innocent detachment from the crimes, and yet with such an intense belief in the emotions of the motives that had brought those crimes about. Clearly the massacre of the strangers had been for me more than just the telling of a story. For once in my life I had not been constrained by the severe discipline of history, but had been at liberty to invoke the dilemmas inscribed in my own heart, inscribed there during my childhood, and which had haunted me ever since.

I turned off the water and stepped out of the shower. I had not found a resolution to these dilemmas, of course, but by writing Dougald's story I had found a certain calm, and even a feeling of possibility, in relation to them that I had not known before. Was it that I had at last broken my silence about such things as guilt and innocence and the unreasoning persistence of evil? Now that I had Dougald's reassurance about the worth of my story to him, could I dare to think of it not as something completed but as a modest beginning of something more complex, more ambitious, a larger project altogether that might occupy me for the rest of my life? The idea excited me. Winifred was the only person who would have understood the powerful claim on me of such a possibility. To a stranger it must have seemed a cheap arrogance. But I was thinking of the carton of mouldering notes on my bookshelves in the study at home. I was not thinking, *I will do something with them.* Oh, no. I was just seeing them there. My mind flew to them but did not give me a reason for flying to them, it only gave me the emotion, the feeling of being, at that moment, happy.

After I had dressed I carried one of the hard-backed chairs from the kitchen into the yard and set it by the back door in the shade of the gum tree. I sat on the chair and supported my ankle on the block Dougald used for splitting firewood. The shower had greatly eased the pains and my body throbbed steadily, like an idling motor. When Dougald said to me, in that disbelieving, admiring tone of voice, *You could have been there*, they were the sweetest words I had ever heard. For, of course, I *had* been there. But only I knew that.

* * *

* * *

It was a week later and Dougald had been working all day on the engine of the truck. He was getting the truck ready for our journey south into the escarpments of the Expedition Range. He was determined to make the trip, but was nervous and anxious about this return to his country after such a long absence from it. That night I believe his habitual calm failed him. I lay awake listening to him traipsing around the house, the claws of his bitch tap-tapping on the boards, as if a blind harbinger announced him in his nocturnal wanderings.

In the morning, the purple caverns of his eyes were darker and more recessed than usual. He told me at breakfast that since reading my story—and he had reread it several times—he had begun to look on this indifferent world of his exile at Mount Nebo with the hope of a return to his own country, and that it made him anxious to be gone as soon as possible. 'I feel as if I'm running out of time, old mate.' I reassured him that he had plenty of time, but I understood his concern. As soon as we have something precious to achieve we begin to fear death, where before we had remained indifferent to it. To go back with assurance now to that place he had dreamed of all his life, that idealised place of his imagination which he had not seen since he was a youth, was a grave and uncertain undertaking for him. And he had never disclosed why he had not gone back sooner. This was to remain a mystery. Even when we are young there is a risk of disillusion in revisiting the scenes of our first joys and despairs. But to return to the place of our youth when we are old is surely to hazard our most cherished dreams. He was determined, however, that he and I would visit together the place of Gnapun's last days. He spoke of it to me several times, his eyes alight with his dream of actually being there. 'We'll do it, old mate,' he said, and must have repeated the mantra of this reassurance a dozen times or more, no doubt in order to convince himself of it as much as to convince me.

In the evening he sat rereading the story. 'Old age is not the time for clambering about among mountainous escarpments,' I reminded him. But he was not to be put off and was proof against my cautioning. 'The truck will get us most of the way,' he said, not looking up from his reading. 'It's only a bit of a hike from the river. You'll see.'

While I was washing the breakfast dishes the next morning he returned from feeding the hens and brought me a fine knobbed cane. 'Here,' he said, handing it to me as if it were the answer to my misgivings about our proposed journey to the Expedition Range. 'It belonged to my mother. It was in the cottage.' He stood and watched while I stepped across the kitchen with it. My gait fell with a surprising naturalness into a pivoting of the hips and a rolling of the shoulders that was not unlike the action of my uncle's gait. 'You look like you've never been without it,' he said approvingly. 'That's just the way Ma used to walk.' So natural to me was the action, indeed, and so effective the stick in taking the weight from my ankle, that I might have been using it for years. In a way I felt myself to be more *me* with it than I had felt without it. The polished globe of the knob fitted familiarly and firmly to my palm, like the reassuring grip of an old friend. I was delighted with it. It was as if I and the stick had been reunited. The rap of the ferule against the boards was a satisfying sound.

I turned at the door and grinned at Dougald, flourishing the stick grandly. 'You see, I am now an old man with a walking stick.' I saw that he had indeed seen just such an image of me. It was a transformation. I felt it. And he saw it. The stick changed me. With it in my hand I ceased to resist old age. I offered Dougald a go but he declined to play the game, no doubt reluctant to appear to me as I appeared to him. I walked about the kitchen some more, and the sound of my uncle stumping about downstairs at night in the farmhouse on his wooden peg was vivid within me.

Expedition Range

17

The demons of the road

Frost glittered on the corrugated iron roofs of the houses as we drove through the township, the three dogs shivering in the back of the truck with our gear. I thought Mount Nebo had never looked so romantic, as if it were a slumbering hamlet on the edge of a Russian forest a century ago. Dougald waved and hooted the horn as we drove past the service station, but I did not see any sign of life there. Esmé was to look in at the house each day and keep an eye on things. She would feed the hens in exchange for the eggs. When she asked Dougald what had happened to the goat he replied without hesitation, 'She got away on us.' He was evidently not afraid of a lie, and had no intention of giving me up.

After we left the last house behind, the road swung south, its red surface spearing through the grey ocean of scrub to the horizon. We sped on, the secret world of the yellow robin rushing past in a blur. Dougald hugged the trembling wheel and said little, keeping the truck to the crown of the gravel, a plume of dust fanning out behind us, his foot hard down on the accelerator.

As we travelled south all that day, seated beside each other in the noisy cabin of the old truck, Dougald's mood became more silent and inward and he was not responsive to my attempts at conversation. No doubt he was meditating on what lay ahead of us. It was a moment of great uncertainty for him. The countryside we drove through was unchanging and uninhabited. I saw no cattle or wild animals and we encountered no traffic.

I once drove through the forest with my uncle in his truck all one wintry day, when the late wartime country-side of Germany possessed just such an appearance of austere melancholy and abandonment, its only occupants seemingly ourselves in the speeding truck, the trees rushing past and the wind roaring at the windows. It was a landscape in mourning, and that is how I think of it still, that country of the past to which my soul belongs. My uncle's features were set that day in the mask he often wore of forever reaching into himself for something final, some elusive thing that he could never quite lay his hand to, hoping and longing for a sudden illuminating sign that would confirm his need to be at one with his earth. Not the land, not quite the *country* the way Dougald spoke of it, but the deep, black, arable earth that his father had fed and enriched and *his* father before him. How his silence during that drive, the expression that was confirmed on his features, spoke to me of his anxiety to draw me into his religion of the earth and to baptise me with its sacred torments. It was his principal preoccupation while I was with him, how this might be accomplished. His passion, his jealousy of my father, his brooding loneliness, his despairing knowledge that the search for the spiritual is always elsewhere, had driven him down into himself until he had lost sight of the world. He was not a man of the city, but was a man whose mind remained closed, a man whose obsession drew him into a solitary place where he could no longer be reached by others. And it might have been that his arms flew up out of that lonely place and he cried out to me, beseeching me, that I, his nephew, his *only* nephew, the son of his sister, would hear him and would at the last reach down to him and take hold of his hands and be at one with him in his final years, and that for this betrothal to the soil of my ancestors I would renounce my own father.

We camped that night, my uncle and I, by a cold stream at the edge of the forest, and in the night I heard him knocking on his wooden leg. I more than half-believed he tapped a message to a spirit presence with whom he held sinister communion. *Your father is not at the front*, he murmured to me, the madness of belief in his blue eyes. *He is engaged upon secret work.* Had he tried he might have won me with love, but he was no longer capable of love. He could not win me with fear and enmity. The seed of fear and doubt he sowed in me against my father set him apart from me in a world of his own that I could not have entered even if I had desired to, for I loved my father. My uncle's fierce despair was founded in his knowledge that his earth was to die with him. That was the vision that haunted him, just as Dougald had been haunted by the thought that Gnapun's story would be lost forever when he died. There was a fear of extinction in both their dreams. My uncle knew that no one would replace him in his priestly dedication to the wellbeing of his soil when he was gone. And he was right. He foresaw the end of his meaning. Today there are vast suburbs where he grew his crops and grazed his sheep and cows, and he and his ways and his peculiar obsessions are unknown by the people who live in those suburbs. It all ended. Everything. Nothing of him, nothing of his house or his ideas, not a thing of it remains, except my own doubt about the decency of my father that he seeded in me, and which found its sustenance in my childhood fears and took root there, growing within me as I grew, drawing its canopy of silence over me like the canopy of a great dark tree that my uncle had planted at the edge of his fields in a moment of despair and bitterness.

I have lived my life within the shadow of this doubt. I have been unable to *know*, certain one moment of my father's goodness, and the next as certain of his guilt—to *sense* the atrocious participation of his hands that had held me with love. When I was a boy during the war there was much I could not know, but I knew, as everyone knew, that an evil beyond the reckoning of humanity was being done in our names and that we were never to understand it or to recover from it. It has haunted my generation and the ghost of it will not be gone until we are gone. A capacity for deep silence was revealed within each of us, like a cavern we had not known to exist before. No matter how lofty our moral principles, few of us proved immune to the pernicious charms of silence. My mother, my father, my sister and I. We all kept our silence. We children were crippled by it and lost our voices to it. No doubt people *will* forget, one day, eventually. And of course there are those brave and gifted souls who do find their voices. I wonder sometimes if Katriona, living her life in London with her English husband, has already begun to forget. And *her* children. Will they even be told? But one lifetime is not long enough to forget. One lifetime is not time enough for anything much at all.

I looked across at Dougald, where he sat hunched over the wheel beside me, glowering at the endless road that seemed to stand, vertical and stationary, before us, as if it were a great porphyry obelisk denying us entry into the landscape instead of providing us with a way forward. With his gift of the story of his great-grandfather, Dougald had unknowingly instructed me in my own way forward. I had asked myself since then if it was too late for me to go back and to search the records for my father's war service. Was it too late for me to write my fiction of his life? For what else might it become but a fiction? I could never again pretend to a sufficient objectivity to write the story of my father's life and times as history. I had failed at history, and there was no point returning to it. Suppose I uncovered the worst? What then? What if the facts of my father's story were so dire they refused to yield to the poetics of fiction? Perhaps some things cannot be, and should not be, written as fiction. Perhaps it is only with the detached gravitas of historical scholarship, with words based upon the undeniable facts of documentary records and eyewitness accounts, that some things can be set before the generations that follow us. Perhaps fiction dissolves the pain too readily, and too readily enables us to accept and to absolve ourselves. Acceptance is surely an early stage of forgetting. I had already begun to accept the reality of Winifred's death, and was this acceptance not the beginning of forgetting the grief of my loss? But we cannot go on accumulating griefs on griefs. Writing the story of Gnapun's terrible deeds I put on the mask and danced, and the dance exhilarated me. Eventually we accept the ghosts that haunt us and we become their familiars, at which they lose their terrors for us and are soon our playthings. But to make a fiction of the deeds of the generation of my father must inevitably be to humanise those deeds and to betray the truth of what was inhuman, not to preserve it. Perhaps only history can preserve it. So what then, I wondered, had I done with

Gnapun's story if I had not humanised the motives of the perpetrators of the massacre? I needed, I realised, to reread the story in order to know what I had done. To have done it was one thing, but to know what it was that I had done was another. Perhaps I would wish to destroy it when I read it. Was it mine to destroy? Who owned the story now, Dougald or me? Or was it the property of us both? The story satisfied him. It delighted him. It was what he wanted from me. It fulfilled his dream of a continuation. He was possessive of it. He had not returned my journal, but told me he would return it to me once he had entered the story on his computer. But I had seen no sign of him beginning to do this.

As we rattled on along that road all day, my doubts and uncertainties circled around in my head like insistent crows over a cornfield. Suppose one day the descendants of those massacred innocents should come upon my story and see in it a celebration of what had taken place? The thought chilled me. Might it be enough for them that I acknowledged the brotherhood of Gnapun and the leader of the strangers, and that I had seen a biblical parallel in the murder of one brother by the other? I turned to Dougald and shouted above the din of the rattling cabin, 'Did you bring my journal?'

He did not respond, but gazed down the road like a blind man. So engrossed, so hypnotised was he by the road, he might have forgotten I was beside him. I longed to escape from the vibrating cabin and to stand alone in the stillness of the scrub and to be face to face once again with the fearless, inquiring eye of the yellow robin. For where else but in such creatures can we find the certainty of innocence?

18

Wylah

Late in the afternoon Dougald pulled up in a small town and bought some stores. Before leaving the town we ate a meal in the only café there. The man who served us was Greek and spoke scarcely two words of English. I asked him which island he was from but he did not understand my question. I have never encountered a living soul who seemed to me to be further from his home than this man. He sat on a stool behind his counter and smoked one cigarette after another. His features were without expression as he watched us eat our meal. It was as if he watched the sea at his door. When he saw that we had finished eating he stubbed out his cigarette and walked over to us and collected our dishes without a word, then returned to his dreaming solitude behind the counter and lit another cigarette. Dougald and I were his only customers. We might have been the only customers he had ever had. When we had eaten I thanked him and we drove on. Soon it was as if the town had never existed. I remarked to Dougald, 'That Greek is a true exile.' I felt for the fate of the man, as it seemed to touch something in all of us. Dougald said nothing to this. He was preoccupied, his thoughts no doubt far ahead of us in his own country.

I dozed for a time after our meal and when I opened my eyes we had left the scrub behind and were passing through a landscape of vast open downs on which crops had recently been sown. In the distance the ramparts of great cliffs rose abruptly from the plain. Rising behind the cliffs were the soft outlines of a range of wooded mountains and steep valleys. When we came to within a few kilometres of the cliffs, Dougald gave up his anxious embrace of the wheel and squared his shoulders, and he rested against the back of his seat, as if he were satisfied at last that the view before him was not a mirage but was real and would not disappear as we drew close to it, but would soon resolve faithfully into its familiar details.

He lifted his hand and pointed. 'There she is, old mate,' he said. 'The Expedition Range.' He described with his outspread fingers the silvery lines that lay along the flanks of the great rock walls. 'They are waterfalls,' he said. 'They've had good rains down this way.' He spoke as if there had been no tension between us. I looked across at him and he turned to me and smiled, a youthful delight in his eyes. 'This is it, old mate,' he said.

I saw how moved he was to see his country once again, and I envied him this reunion with his past and wondered how I might have felt if such a reunion were possible for me. There was, of course, no place such as this that I might return to. Hamburg today is not the city in which I was born, nor is it the place where I grew up, but is a new construction, and the strange and beautiful countryside where my uncle had his farm, and where I encountered the gipsy girl, is no longer countryside but has been transformed into suburban streets and schools and playgrounds and small, mean strips of parkland that are supposed to have preserved something of the countryside for the new inhabitants but which really are no more than a parody of preservation. The sacred hazel coppice of my childhood has long since been covered by concrete and asphalt.

Seeing the look in Dougald's eyes as he recognised the place of his own boyhood, I understood what a unique privilege it was for him to experience the reassurance of this return after half a century to a country unaltered by time and war and the developments of the twentieth century. It was still the country of his Old People, as he called his ancestors, the term familiar and intimate, as if they were not remote beings whose individual features had been forgotten long ago, but were known to him, and were a people still in occupation of their lands. It was a term that seemed to suggest that the entire colonial enterprise might never have taken place, and that the old reality, like the Old People themselves, had not become extinct but had defied our belief in history and had survived. The Old People, indeed, suggested to me another way altogether of looking at reality and the passage of time than my own familiar historical sense of things, in which change and the fragmentation of epochs and experience is the only certainty.

The waterfalls did not reach the ground but joined together and became a pale drift of mist as they descen-
ded, riding across the face of the cliffs like clouds of smoke, glowing pink and orange in the late afternoon sun, touched here and there by the delicate hues of rainbows,

the whole scene altering as I observed it. As we drew close to the cliffs Dougald slowed and turned off the narrow dirt road. He eased the truck across a cattle grid and drove on in low gear, at little more than a walking pace, following a meander of half-buried wheel ruts through open woodland towards the base of the stone ramparts. We were soon crossing a meadow dotted about with graceful trees, their black trunks and spreading canopies of slender leaves casting a delicate lacework of shadows on the untrodden grass. These stately trees might have been planted to grace the estate of a landowner hundreds of years in the past. Dougald raised his hand and pointed to them. 'Here's your ironbarks, old mate.'

'So this is it then?' I said, for he clearly meant me to understand that this was the meadow Gnapun had crossed that early morning, striding through the ground mist on his way to meet the messengers. I was about to say more when he laid his hand on my shoulder, silencing me. He brought the truck to a halt and switched off the motor. He sat at the wheel in the silence examining the country to our left, his lips parted and his eyes narrowed, as if he anticipated something. I followed the direction of his gaze. A hundred metres or so in that direction the grassland ended abruptly and a forest of tall cinnamon-coloured trees began. These tall, elegant trees were evidently unrelated to the ironbarks of the open woodland through which we had been passing. The valley had narrowed around us and we were enclosed now by the naked rock of the grand escarpments. The crimson and purple granite of the cliffs stated the dominance of these stone presences in this picturesque valley as confidently as if they had been the fortress walls of a medieval lord. I was reminded of the towering stones of the fortified acropolis at Lindos, beneath whose vertiginous buttresses I stood in awe with my father in 1948, when I was a boy of twelve. It was the first time I had visited an ancient site of human worship and refuge. Indeed it was the moment I discovered history. Those monumental antique walls, which seemed wedded to the native rock, had awoken in me a longing to become familiar with the mysteries of our human story, and after my father and I returned to our pension that night I told him, *I am going to be a historian when I grow up.* I can still see my father's joy. Although he was an engineer, no man I have ever met loved to read history more than my father did. Oswald Spengler's peculiar and now long-forgotten volume, *The Decline of the West*, served my father as his Bible, and remained for him throughout his life a consolation to his private disillusion.

Dougald raised his hand and pointed dramatically towards the trees. 'Old Wylah!' There was excitement and relief in his voice. 'See that old fella?'

A large black bird, fully the size of an eagle, detached itself from the topmost branch of the tallest of the cinnamon trees and fell towards the ground in a tumbling flight, like a falling umbrella, flashes of yellow from the undersides of its tail feathers semaphoring as it turned this way then that. Its wailing cry reached us through the silence then; *kee-aah, kee-aah,* it went, echoing from the cliffs and lingering in the air after the bird itself had vanished from our sight. With a thrill I knew that I had heard the sound of Gnapun's signal to his men to strike the death blow against those doomed settlers. I saw the scene that day, the leader's wife standing by the trellis in the garden looking off towards the clouds that bloomed above the hills, her dark hair shining in the sunlight, the blue ribbon in her hat lifting in the breeze, then settling back and resting on the flowers of her dress. It was Winifred I saw, and she was young and beautiful and in love. I realised Dougald was watching me. I said, 'So that was him then?' I had readily acknowledged the cry of the falling bird as Dougald's welcome to his country. It was in Dougald that I witnessed the truth of this, not in myself. I began to understand from that moment that he had needed me to be with him there in the country of his Old People in order to bear witness to his truth. I could see in his happiness how his great-grandfather's welcome offered him the spiritual comfort he had longed for during his years of exile, and how it permitted him to know himself to be truly at home once again. It was a great moment for Dougald. One of those moments in our lives when things turn out exactly as we had hoped they would. Wylah's cry of welcome restored to Dougald a former state of confidence and wellbeing, and from this moment on his manner was for some time more youthful and more self-assured than I had ever known it to be during my brief acquaintance with him.

'That was him, old mate,' he said.

My uncle might have known something of Dougald's emotion at this moment of his reunion with his country. But no one from the city, no worker with the mind, no one who had dealt in the currency of unbelief as I had all of my adult life, could have known the restoration of wellbeing Dougald knew just then.

We sat for a time, silent with each other, looking through the windscreen of the cabin towards the base of the trees where we had seen the falling bird. At last

Dougald started the motor and drove off the trail and through the untracked grass to the edge of the timber. When he had manoeuvred the truck closely in among the trees, he switched off the motor. 'Me and Grandfather camped here while we fenced this place,' he said, as if he imparted the most ordinary kind of information to me, the emotion of his arrival behind him now. 'We lived here for a year.' He gestured at the meadow behind us and towards the valley where it slid narrowly between the cliffs. 'We split fence posts all through here.' He pointed. 'See that stump? Me and Grandad sawed that old ironbark one fine morning and split more than a hundred posts out of her before lunch.' He looked at me and grinned. He seemed capable of splitting a hundred posts before lunch again if he had a mind to do it. 'We'll have a drink of tea before we set up camp,' he said, and he opened his door and stepped down from the cabin. He paused and looked up at me. 'How's that ankle holding up?'

'It's fine,' I said. It wasn't, but I was not going to complain. I looked down at him and thought of how he must have been as a boy here, big and strong and willing, working alongside his grandfather, the violent days of his own father behind him. Setting the knob of my walking stick in the palm of my hand, I opened the door and stepped to the ground. The stick had become a welcome new part of me. I liked it. I liked the feel of it. Once safely down I stood and breathed the sweet cool air and leaned on my stick. There was a sound of water tumbling over stones. As I stood there listening, it seemed to be the very sound, I swear, of the voices of schoolgirls in a glade confiding secrets to one another. I was moved and astonished to find myself alone with this man in such a place so late in my life. I wanted to know the names of the trees and shrubs and grasses, the flowers and the birds, and it seemed to me just then that it would have been a grand thing to be a familiar of this place. My two brown dogs were making off across Gnapun's meadow in pursuit of something, their rumps bouncing along. They were happy dogs. I whistled to them and they paused and looked back at me a moment then ran on. There was the sudden intense smell of wood smoke. I turned to see Dougald squatting by a crackling pile of sticks. He was like a boy on holiday. I hoped my ankle would not let us down tomorrow when we were to climb into the escarpment.

19

Visitors

Dougald picked up his haversack and shrugged into it, his head to one side as he adjusted the straps. In the darkness he looked like a woman adjusting the straps of her brassiere. It was one of those old khaki packs sold in army surplus stores the world over. 'It will be light soon,' he said, and with that he set off. I lurched after him.

We crossed the river where the water ran shallowly over a wide stretch of stones. This morning it did not gossip but murmured privately to itself—of secret things, perhaps, or even prayers to strange gods. It was the ghostly form of his bitch I followed, not him. He had quickly merged with the deep shadows of the far bank. My old town shoes were soaked at once, and I slipped and tottered on the smooth stones, flailing his mother's stick wildly in the air as I struggled to keep myself from falling into the water. I came out of the river behind the bitch and started up the sandy incline. The stick was more use to me here. I planted it in the resistant sand and it took my weight loyally as I heaved myself upward, my shoes squelching and filling with sand. By the time I made it to the top of the bank Dougald had already disappeared in among the solid shadows of the trees, his shape there a moment then gone. I stumbled forward into the trees, trusting I was still on the right path, brushing aside the small branches and ducking under the large ones. A moment later I came out of the trees and there he was ahead of me, standing looking up at the escarpment. I was breathing heavily and wondering at my chances of staying the distance. The way forward was barred by a sheer rock face of grey stone.

'We're not climbing *that*,' I said as I came up to him. We might have been pilgrims arrived at the wall of a fortress. Was this as far as we would go? I asked myself, did Dougald really remember his way about this country, or had he already taken a wrong turn?

He murmured something that I did not catch and began picking his way with care along the base of the cliff. Great tumbled rocks lay about everywhere. I followed him with difficulty, greatly concerned that I would utterly destroy my injured ankle at any moment. I would have liked to stop to empty the water and sand from my socks and shoes, but I was afraid to pause in case I lost sight of him.

As I struggled along behind him through the violet shadows of that dawn, I found myself, for some reason, thinking angrily of my visit to Katriona in London before I flew out to Sydney to attend Vita's conference. I had taken Vita's advice and gone over to England to spend Christmas with my grandchildren. It was a mistake. Reginald, Katriona's husband, was strict with the children and the first night I was with them he packed them off to bed without a story, so that we three adults might eat a small roast leg of New Zealand lamb in peace together in the living room of their grim little flat in Hampstead. The evening was not going well. I had brought an expensive bottle of seven-year-old Montrachet with me but it had not appeared at the table. The man—I mean Reginald, my daughter's husband—was so dismissive of his children I wondered why he had bothered to have them.

When I mentioned that I would be visiting Australia he said disdainfully, not addressing me directly but chewing on a mouthful of meat and apparently addressing a wider audience whose sympathies he was certain of, 'There's nothing interesting in Australia. You'll hate it.' I considered him, then ventured that I hoped this would not prove to be the case. He snorted and fed himself another forkful of meat. Feeling a little provoked by his manner, I asked him if he had visited Australia himself, and was it from this experience that he knew the country to be not worth visiting?

He laughed scornfully, as if such a question insulted his intelligence, and said he would not waste his time going there. 'There are better places than Australia to go if you want to travel. You and Winifred were always talking about spending a year in Venice after you retired.' At this point he paused in his eating and did finally look at me, not meeting my eyes exactly, but casting his supercilious glance *over* me, while at the same time picking with his fingernail at a shred of meat that was lodged between his teeth. 'Why don't you join a tour to Venice?' he said. 'You might meet someone.'

To my dismay Katriona urged me to do as he suggested, claiming that a female companion would help me to recover my spirits. I wondered at Katriona's betrayal of her mother's memory. We speak in order to be understood, and I felt that if I spoke of my private feelings at that moment I was certain to be misunderstood, so I said nothing. I experienced, however, a strong protective impulse towards Australia on Vita's behalf.

Dougald and his pale bitch were nowhere to be seen.

I stopped and stood looking around me in alarm, gripped by the certainty that without Dougald to guide me I was lost in this maze of tumbled stone and crisscross of fallen tree limbs. The wall of the escarpment stood in deep shadow close on my left hand. I called Dougald's name and his voice came back to me at once, softly from the darkness. 'Over here, old mate.' I floundered across to him. He was standing within a gap in the wall of rock. He put a steadying hand to my shoulder. 'Are you okay there?' I apologised for holding him up and explained the problem with my shoes. I was trembling, and was ashamed that I had very nearly panicked. I was tempted to tell him that this excursion was not for me and that he should go on alone and let me find my way back to the truck. I had not foreseen quite how daunting and alien to me the bush would be. He pressed my shoulder encouragingly and said my shoes would soon dry, and he

turned and went on. I followed him. I reassured myself
with the thought that perhaps, after all, we did not have
far to go.

We entered a narrow defile, which sectioned the
cliff. The incline within this passageway became steeper
as we ascended it, and I was soon breathing hard with
the unaccustomed exertion. His mother's stick was a
great support and I was very glad to have it, but even so I
was forced to stop every few yards to catch my breath.
Also the calf muscles in my legs were burning from the
unnatural strain of trying to prevent the smooth soles of
my shoes from slipping back on the loose ground at each
upward step.

I emerged, at last, from between the walls of the
narrow defile onto a flat shelf of land which resembled a
terrace of the Inca. Dawn was breaking over the scene, the
rocks and trees lit by a soft play of golden light. Dougald
had not waited for me but had already crossed the terrace
and was standing looking up at another sheer rock wall
on the far side of it. I was surprised by his energy and
agility. I turned and looked down the way we had come.
The tall cinnamon trees beside the river were far below
us, the meadows of Gnapun spread out in the pale dawn
light, dotted about with the elegant ironbarks. It was as

if I looked down on the artfully designed park of a great country estate. There were no signs of human occupation in the valley, however, no houses or roads, no grazing cattle or sheep, but only the countryside itself, still and silent as it always seems to be; a silence in which the air trembles with a kind of absence, as if the landscape listens, or waits for something. But nothing happens. It is strange and uncanny, this sense of waiting, and it is unsettling. Certainty is withheld as one is led to a sense of expectation, and one is made to suspect that one's perceptions are provisional and will soon require revising. Leichhardt noticed it and found the stars reassuring. He knew himself to be the first European to pass this way on his desperate journey. I began to wonder if I were to be the last. Surely no others but Gnapun and his people had ever made their way among these hidden roads?

I hurried after Dougald. It struck me that I was never going to be quite me again after this. It seemed a great insight at the time, though now that I look back on it I wonder what I thought I meant by it. How would I relate this journey to Reginald, and would he be impressed or would he scoff at my silliness? I didn't care . . . I *did* care, actually. It is a great annoyance that we care for the opinions of people whom we despise. But there, we do.

We continued to gain height, reaching one terrace after another by means of these great cracks and hidden ways within the rock walls. We left the river and the valley far below us, and eventually lost sight of them altogether. We may even have crossed a ridge, or even two ridges, and it may be that the valleys I caught glimpses of far below us from time to time later in the day did not include the valley from which we had begun our ascent that morning. It was not many hours before I no longer knew where I was in relation to where we had started from. And as to our direction, I was bewildered, except that I knew it to be generally upward. Whatever the reality might turn out to be, our destination remained for me the version of Gnapun's rock shelter I had briefly described at the beginning of 'Massacre', and I imagined it up there ahead of us somewhere among the cliffs of the escarpment. In a way, I could not believe it was really there or that we were actually going to reach it. Gnapun's cave was not a real place for me, but was an image in my imagination, which I had acquired partly from Dougald's original description of it in his story and had partly concocted from my own imagination. There had seemed to me, from the very beginning of this excursion, something a little unnecessary and obsessive in

Dougald's determination that he and I must actually go together to visit the real cave. But of course I did not feel the need of it that he did. I don't think it is too much to claim that for Dougald this journey was a pilgrimage—a last pilgrimage—to the spiritual centre of his life. And if it was not that exactly, then it was something just as important as that. No equivalent place existed for me. Where was the spiritual centre of my life? The question had no meaning for me.

After an hour or two of following him and his tireless bitch I gained a kind of second wind and became more or less inured to the pain in my ankle.

The sun climbed high into a cloudless sky and the day grew warm. The air was fragrant with those mysterious perfumes whose source I had no knowledge of. I sweated and no doubt I groaned aloud every so often when the going was particularly tough. A little after noon by my watch, Dougald called a halt in the shade of a wild cherry tree beside a spring on one of the numerous terraces, and he lit a fire and boiled a billy of water. I sank down onto the soft grass in the shade of the tree beside our little fire and lay on my back. He called me when the tea was ready, and in silence we drank it and ate the entire packet of arrowroot biscuits he had purchased at the Greek's café. I was too tired to talk and had run out of questions. I think by that stage I was feeling rather fatalistic about the outcome of our search for Gnapun.

After resting for little more than half an hour, Dougald packed our few things into his rucksack and stood up. 'You all set there, old mate?' he asked, looking down at me and anxious to be on his way. My joints were stiff after the rest and I struggled to my feet with difficulty and hobbled after him, following him through the confusing world of giant walls and terraces that seemed to go on without end. We came upon well-grassed flats, where we quenched our thirst at springs of clear water that seeped from the ground, and where delicate grass trees and ferns grew in the sweet stillness among the rocks. On one magical occasion it seemed as if we had stepped into a formal Chinese garden, and I forgot my fatigue and imagined a Sung poet seeking this sequestered place to spend his last days meditating upon the foolishness of humankind. But mostly the country was dry and rocky, the trees small, twisted and without character. We walked beside stone ramparts that insisted they had been constructed by iron men. And once I was startled when a group of animals rose suddenly from their siesta and fled at our approach. For an instant I thought they were people. When the sun at last began to decline towards the horizon, we had still not reached Gnapun's cave.

Nature was not everything that day, however. There was something else besides nature, some confusion of the mind, either of mine or of Dougald's, that came by degrees to lie at the centre of this expedition into the heart of the country of his Old People. I am still not sure what happened, but I will do my best to describe it here nevertheless.

It was late in the day and I was resting on a log in the middle of one of these by now familiar terraces, my leg thrust out in front of me, my hip and ankle aching fiercely. I was massaging my thigh with both my hands, for the pain was considerable and was greater once we stopped than it had been while we were walking. My ankle had more or less given way and the pain had inched its way up the side of my leg into my groin. Every time I set my foot on the ground it felt as if someone was digging about in my flesh with a steel needle. The sun was nearing the horizon and I was clammy and chill with my cooling sweat. Bits of twigs and leaves had got down my shirt and were irritating my skin, but I could not be bothered getting them out. It is true, I was an old man and I was tired and it is quite possible I was also a little confused by then. I do not wish to deny it. The day had been a difficult one for me and I was deeply preoccupied by my anxieties about my ankle and whether I would be able to make it back to our camp by the river before nightfall. I had often found myself daydreaming during the day and frequently had lost sight of Dougald and his bitch. This worried me and I knew I was finding it difficult to remain alert to the realities of our situation. Panic flickered at the edges of my reason and I waited with anxiety for its sudden overwhelming onset, as if my panic was to be the beginning of the last act of a tragedy—or was it a comedy? I am prepared to accept some share of responsibility for all this, but I do not believe that I was alone in being the entire cause of it. Delusion is, by its nature, a strange and estranging condition of mind. A part of us knows when we are deluded, but we are nevertheless unable to convince ourselves to act contrary to the dictates of the delusion. It is surely this inability to line ourselves up with what we know to be the realities of our situation that is the trigger for our eventual panic and our downfall.

So there we were at the end of that long and exhausting day, two tired old men high in the escarpments of the wild Expedition Range, searching fruitlessly for a place that one of us had visited in his youth and had not seen since. It was an unlikely affair and there is no doubt that the odds had always been against us in this foolish enterprise. We were too old to be on a quest. Quests are for the young.

I watched Dougald with an increasing feeling of helplessness about our situation. He had lost his earlier confidence some time before this and was now making his way uncertainly across the perfectly flat and almost lawn-like surface of the terrace, which looked as if a gardener had lovingly trimmed it that morning. He was walking unsteadily towards a rocky prominence that jutted out over the valley, like the prow of an old galleon, as if he intended surveying the lower reaches of the escarpment for some familiar sign by which to determine our position before it grew too dark to see. It was the third occasion on which we had returned to this same terrace. Yes, the *third*. I had rested briefly on this same log for the first time hours earlier and had asked him then, 'Where is Gnapun's cave from here? Surely it cannot be far now?' But he did not answer me. As I watched him now I was remembering his words to me of the previous evening. *It's just up here a bit of a way*, he had said, waving his hand carelessly in the general direction of the escarpment. And no doubt when he was a youth, and in the company of his confident grandfather, the journey from the river to Gnapun's cave probably had seemed to be no more than just up here a bit. I watched him weaving around on his way to the edge of the terrace, pausing to look about, then going on a few steps. To me he had the appearance of a man who was lost. But was he lost? How are we to know the truth that is in another's heart? At that moment I accepted what seemed to me to be the unthinkable fact, but a fact nevertheless, that Dougald was lost in the heart of his own country. And it was on this belief that I based my subsequent behaviour. But had I really seen what I thought I had seen? A lost man? Or had I seen a man in a kind of trance? A man in a condition that I had never before witnessed, and which I could not therefore understand or recognise?

I was no longer in the receptive state of mind that I had been in when we arrived at the river the previous evening, when I readily acknowledged the cry of the funereal black cockatoo as a welcome-home call to Dougald from his great-grandfather, Old Wylah, the merciless Gnapun. Now I was tired and irritated, and I was afraid. I had lost confidence in Dougald's plan and was in a sceptical frame of mind. I was no longer a believer. I saw a lost man, and no one, at that moment, could have convinced me otherwise. I did not see a man who believed himself to be in communion with the spirits of his Old People. It was not possible for me to have seen such a thing as that, or to have believed it a likely explanation for Dougald's wandering behaviour. I was not in a mood to consider such things. I just wanted to be reassured that he was going to be able to get us both back to the truck safely, and that we were not going to perish in this wilderness. I did recall—and it was a warning to me that I ignored— that Leichhardt had suffered from a loss of confidence in his leadership by his followers similar to this loss of confidence which Dougald was now suffering from me. And of course Leichhardt also, and on his own admission, had felt at times compelled to go wandering off aimlessly and alone for hours on end, quite as if he had abandoned his senses and his companions and was lost, when in fact he was meditating on the mysterious workings of Providence, in which he had remained a steadfast believer. But, as I said, I ignored this warning. I ignored it because I heard it in the bland, superior voice of my detested other, the one who always behaves sensibly and never gets himself into such awkward scrapes as these.

We dismiss each other, he and I. That is the essence of our relationship, to be dismissive, contemptuous and even loathing of the other. And yet, at some essential level, in the very depths and subsoil of our being, as it were, where we are one and the same person, we share the same beliefs. That is the truth. What more can I say? I would not be without him. And without me, well, he would have no existence at all.

It was on the first occasion of our arrival on this terrace with its log, where I was sitting massaging my aching thigh, that I first observed, with a feeling of alarm, that Dougald had begun to lose the energy of his confidence, and to cast about him uncertainly for the way forward. I almost exclaimed to him then, *My God, Dougald, are you lost?* But the thought was too incredible and I did not dare voice it. His appearance was a dramatic reversal of the previous evening's youthful transformation. The vivid energy that drove him and buoyed his spirits then and in the morning was gone. It happened suddenly. As I looked at him I saw his energy drain out of him and watched with a feeling of horror as he was overtaken by a dazed bewilderment that shone in his eyes, as if he saw ghosts. And who is to say he did not see ghosts? Those who do not see ghosts themselves will no doubt say that Dougald did not see them either. But I do not say that, although I observed the change in him myself with disbelief. Very soon he took on the appearance of a disoriented old man, casting about him first this way then that, standing and gazing vacantly up at the heights, a shocked expression on his face, his mouth agape, his eyes watery and pallid—the very image, indeed, of the old dodderer who had crossed the road in the rain in front of Vita and me—then lowering his eyes and going back over ground that he had gone over twice before, searching for a sign that I was soon convinced was not there to be found. I did not doubt that we were in the wrong place. He did not reply when I suggested this, however, but looked as bewildered and deaf as one who no longer knows what is real and what is delusion. When I spoke to him his gaze passed over me as if he did not see me but saw a shadow, something of a memory that pestered him.

My country is written in my heart, he had said, or some such thing. So had his country disowned him now? Had he returned only to find himself rejected, his dream of home an illusion after all? Had Wylah's welcoming cry been nothing more than a cruel trick to lure him on to his defeat, to show him that without his grandfather he was not a familiar here, but was a man unknown to the Old People of his vanished clan after all? Was he to know himself to be an outcast? An exile here too? This was, I believed at the time, what he was experiencing during this strange episode of bewilderment. I began to feel a deep sorrow for his suffering and I wanted nothing more than to restore him to his former belief. This was the terrible blow that had waited for him all those years in the escarpments of the Expedition Range and which, within an hour, had made of him a broken man. That was the view I came to as I sat there watching him. He had been cast out from his country and was lost. How else was I to see it?

It was with a feeling of relief about myself then that I realised, without needing to debate the matter, that I was not going to abandon him but was going to stick by him, and that if it came to it I would prefer to perish with him there on Gnapun's mountain than make the attempt to save myself. It was an enormous relief to know this. It was a joy. It made me happy to know it. When the end came I would hold him in my arms while he wept for his loss, just as he had held me in his arms that night at the Nebo River while I wept for my loss. He was a bewildered old man and he needed his friend at his side.

I gripped my thigh with both hands and, setting myself

to struggle to my feet, I looked up. He was gone! He and his bitch. I let go of my thigh and grasped his mother's stick, put my weight on it and stood. I groaned aloud as the pain flashed through me. There was no sign of them. I stumped across the terrace to where the rock prow jutted out over the valley and, stepping to the edge, leaned and looked down. A jumble of great stones and thorny plants greeted my eye. There was no sign of him. I turned and looked about me. Standing there, it seemed to me that the peculiar waiting silence of the bush would soon bring my every belief into question. I could hear it, a creaking, a kind of singing in the air. What was it waiting *for*? I called his name aloud. 'Dougald!' My voice called back to me, once, twice, then faint and failing into the valley. Professor Max Otto calling in the wilderness. I called again more boldly. 'Dou-gaaald!' There was no reply, except the echo of my own voice. I could make no impression on the silence. The world in which I stood had been there forever. Soon I would be gone and nothing would have changed. It seemed foolish to call to him again. I had seen how old men decline and die with a suddenness that takes us by surprise. Hadn't I seen my father become a lost child in the last days before his death? He had seemed innocent then at last in his childish happiness when I smiled at him and held his hand in mine. Had he been comforted and consoled by the presence of his son?

As I stood there at the edge of the terrace I willed Dougald to reappear in front of me. We would sit side by side on the log and rest a while. I would light a fire and brew another pannikin of tea. *If we don't find the cave today*, I would say cheerily, *then we can return and search for it again tomorrow*. But this was nonsense. It was gibberish. I knew it for what it was. Either we were to find Gnapun's cave today or we were never to find it. That had always been the reality. I do not know how long I had been standing there thinking about these things, when suddenly a dizziness passed over me and I swayed, leaning and pivoting on my stick, and was forced to take a quick step forward in order to prevent myself from falling. For an instant, teetering on the brink of that rocky prominence, it seemed possible that Dougald had ceased to imagine me and that I had therefore vanished from his landscape and that I stood in another, a place unknown to him. I knew this not to be a sensible thought, but it possessed nevertheless a quite compelling reality for me. I tottered back to the log, my one certain point of reference, and I lowered myself onto it with care. I would wait for him. He would return eventually and explain his absence. I did not know what to think of my situation. I closed my eyes. I had not minded the idea of dying with Dougald in my arms. There had seemed to be some point to that for both of us. But I did not want to die here in the escarpment on my own. I rested my arms on my knees and held my head in my hands. Somewhere far off a dog howled. I lifted my head and listened. Was it one of my dogs? They had been missing all day. Or was his bitch calling to me? Had he fallen and was he lying helpless and injured somewhere among the rocks?

Dusk was rapidly closing on the terrace now. I fancied I could hear a faint whispering nearby. Violet and purple shadows billowed around me like clouds, the air suddenly cold and shifting. I shivered. Then I realised what the whispering was and looked up. A gilded speck lanced through the sky far above me, leaving its white trail. I thought of the people in their seats, eating those meals that we are forced to eat and watching films that we would not otherwise watch. The faint whispering set the air trembling delicately around me. I looked again at the place where I had last seen him, willing myself to believe he would soon reappear and come towards me, waving cheerfully and calling to me to come on and to follow him, his confidence restored. The howling of a dog again broke the silence. It was distant, possibly even in the valley far below, holding to a flute-like note, then dying away, only to rise again. It was a beautiful and melancholy sound, almost the sound of a lamentation. If he had fallen and injured himself, then the sooner I found him the better. If I were to leave it too long before setting out after him I might not find him alive. If he were dying and in pain he would need my comfort. But to go in search of him in the dark would be to panic. That is the form panic would take, rushing off into the dark and calling his name. I decided to give him another quarter-hour by my watch. If he had not returned by then, by the precise and reckoned time of watches and clocks and not by the insistent urgency of the panic that was gathering in me, then I would go and look for him. I would go carefully and steadily, making certain of my bearings as I moved from one place to the next. And I would call his name every so often, then stand in the stillness and listen for his answering call. And sooner or later, if I were careful and methodical in my search, I would find him. He was here somewhere. He could not be far away.

When I checked my watch the quarter-hour I had allowed had already passed. But still I did not get up off the log. I had a dread of what I might find, and a greater dread that I might not find anything at all and would be confronted with the bleakest prospect. But to do nothing and to just sit here waiting would be a miserable and a cowardly way to end this thing. How would it sound in my book of account? *I waited.* I do not know how long I had been sitting there musing on my situation, when it occurred to me that Dougald had forgotten me. *He has forgotten you*, said the voice of my superior other, my ever-rational brother. Old men forget, it was true. *How* they forget. Dougald had not fallen over the edge of the terrace, and he could not have climbed the cliff at my back, so he must have gone down through the copse of stunted trees directly in front of me and to the left of the prow, forgetting that he was leaving me behind. I must follow him at once, or there would be no hope of ever catching up with him.

I got to my feet and stumped across the grass towards the dark silhouettes of the copse, planting my stick and swinging my hips as if I was my uncle out in the night in search of straying cattle. There was no track or any indication of a possible trail. Once I had got in among the bushes I clambered about aimlessly, lashing out with my stick at the prickly branches. The bushes grew lower to the ground and were more dense as I descended the slope, and I made headway with great difficulty. Then, in one step, I was out of it. I was standing on the stony bed of a dry creek. The bushes and creepers through which I had been clambering overhung the creek and formed a kind of canopy or tunnel. Crouching, and in pain, I made my way forward. I had been going along in this manner for some time, so preoccupied with my progress that I had more or less forgotten that I was supposed to be following Dougald, when I lost my footing and fell violently over an abrupt drop of several feet.

I lay on my back on a mattress of flood debris, winded and too confused and exhausted to make the effort to get up. I closed my eyes and rested. I was not too uncomfortable so long as I did not attempt to move. Astonishingly I was still clutching my stick. It seemed a triumph to have retained my grip on it. I think I must have gone to sleep then, for some time later during that night Winifred came to me. I was enormously grateful and was astonished to see her. I said, 'Oh, Christ, is it really you my darling?' I laughed and wept with relief to see her standing there just above me and to the left—for some reason her precise position was important to me. So, from the very beginning, had this all been nothing but an elaborate dream? She did not speak or try to reach me, however, but stood looking down at me silently from her slightly superior position. It dawned on me then that she was actually taking her final leave of me and was gazing sorrowfully into the coffin of her beloved husband. So I had died before she had? Just as we had expected me to. I noticed then that my father was standing behind her in the shadows. One of his hands was resting on her shoulder, as if he wished to comfort her, or to make the point that he stood with her at this moment. The sight of my father standing there in the shadows made me begin to suspect that they were not real. Why could Winifred not have come to see me on her own? I did not want to see my father. They stood looking down at me and gradually, as I watched them, I ceased to believe in them and they faded away.

When I woke again I smelled smoke and saw the gipsy girl clambering up the side of the creek. She was just leaving. Had she lit a fire for me? Surely she had been watching over me? I called to her, 'Please don't leave! Tell me your name!' But she paid no heed and was soon gone among the dark foliage of the trees. 'You are not forgotten!' I called. 'Your courage is not forgotten.' Tears ran down my cheeks. We were only children, she and I, but we had known everything there is to know; all that we were and all that we had ever been was contained for us in our meeting that day in the hazel coppice. I knew this with absolute surety. I *understood* it. It was not Winifred and the decades of our companioned lives, not my years of teaching, not my friendships with colleagues and students, not my father and mother, it was the enigma of my meeting with the gipsy girl in the hazel coppice that golden evening of my boyhood. It was that I valued more than anything else in my whole life. Within the brief circle of my meeting with her, the prophetic significance of my entire existence had been portrayed. Understanding this, I was suddenly content to die there alone in this remote escarpment of the Expedition Range. It was not such a strange place after all. Lying there on my back on the stones and roots of Gnapun's mountain that night, my recollection of my meeting with the gipsy girl was more consolation to me than all the rest of it. Though why this should have been so, I cannot truthfully say now as I sit here reflecting on the events of that night. I knew it in my heart, let us say, where our knowing, as I have said before, is of another kind. I did not mind this death. To lie up here with the bones of Gnapun was not such a terrible thing. I was as much at home with him as with anyone. I was a man, as he had been. In a way, he was my hero too. We all die, after all, it is the least reducible fact of our existence. I regretted only that I had not known her name. It was my one regret that I could not at this last speak the name of the gipsy girl aloud to myself.

I woke to the touch of a cool rough tongue on my cheek. I opened my eyes. Dougald's wolf-like bitch licked my face, her grey eyes gazing steadily into mine. Behind her head a disc of silver slid between the trees, touching the rocks with its aluminium light—it was Gnapun's awakening! I laughed at the excess of this thought and reached and drew her shoulder against me. She was trembling and I could feel her rapid heartbeat through her ribs. While I struggled to my feet she stood looking on, waiting for me. We did not have far to go.

'You know where you are now, old mate,' Dougald called cheerfully as I came up to him. It evidently amused him that he'd had to send his bitch to fetch me. He squatted by a small fire alongside the log on the terrace, his features ruddy in the flames, the sky behind him the palest saffron with the approaching dawn. 'Me and Grandad spent the night here beside this log, paying our respects, before we visited Gnapun.' He twisted around and pointed to the cliff at the edge of the terrace behind him. 'We'll go up there when we've had this drink of tea.'

I stood looking down at him. He was himself again, the firelight flickering on his dark features, his eyes alight and youthful, his vigour recomposed within him. He poured steaming tea from the billy into a mug and stirred in sugar and handed it up to me.

I took the mug and thanked him and drank from it.

He looked narrowly into my eyes. 'Pity we ate all them arrowroot biscuits,' he said and leaned forward to tend the fire, finding small sticks and poking them in under the billy, which he had set to boil again.

I sat on the log and cupped my hands around the hot mug and sipped the sweet tea and I closed my eyes. After a while I opened them. He was watching me. I said, 'I had visitors last night.'

He nodded solemnly. 'Well that's good, old mate.'

I was grateful there was no hint of irony in his tone. I waited for him to speak of his own visitors, but he said no more and looked into the fire.

When it was light I followed him around the base of the cliff. There was a natural cutting in the rock wall which formed a gentle incline like a ramp. He stopped ahead of me on a narrow shelf ten or twelve metres above our campsite and waited for me to draw level with him.

It was obvious the moment I saw it. A dry stone wall was built into the face of the low cliff. It was such a considered, man-made feature in that otherwise entirely natural landscape that its presence was as startling, and as beautiful and mysterious in its way, as the ruins of an ancient temple. Seeing it there, it was possible to imagine strange gods. Dougald said nothing, but turned to me as I came up to him and put his arm around my shoulders. I was moved by this unaccustomed intimacy.

'I would never have come back here on my own,' he said. He left his arm around my shoulders, and we stood together thus, looking at the stone wall in the deep quiet of that wilderness, the morning chorus of birds far below us in the valley. 'My grandfather set up this wall to protect his father's bones. The day he brought me here I saw it for the first time as you see it now. It is just as I have seen it in my memory since.' He laughed softly, marvelling at the perfect register of his boyhood memory with the intact wall in front of us. 'All my life,' he said with a kind of wonder, 'I have been able to close my eyes and to count every one of those stones.' He turned and examined me. 'Me and Grandad looked into the cave, then we set each of them stones back in place before we left here fifty years ago.'

He continued to stand with me, looking at the wall. I had begun to think he intended to approach no closer, when he dropped his arm to his side and made his way forward the last few metres. When I hung back he turned and beckoned to me to join him. The stones were flat and long and had been carefully selected. He lifted the topmost of them from its place and handed it to me. 'Set it on its base,' he instructed me, and he watched while I carefully laid the stone on the ground at my feet before he turned and handed me the next. He might have been handing into my care not stones but the precious antique volumes of his library. I thought of the poet's line, *Stones on which there was nothing mortal*. 'They have to go back just the way Grandad set them.' When we had removed three courses of stones down to a level with our chests he reached his arm around my shoulder and drew me towards him and we leaned together and looked into the cavity.

It was a rock shelter rather than a cave. The low ceiling sloped down and met the floor no more than three metres from the entrance. It took a moment for my eyes to adjust to the shadowed interior. The skull was the first thing I saw. A human skull is such a distinctive object that there is no mistaking it for something else. The bones were not so obvious at first. The skeleton was half-buried by an accumulation of debris that had evidently leached from the roof over the years. A tiny black bat, no larger than the final joint of my little finger, clung to the ceiling above the skull, its eyes the bright jewels of a funeral decoration. Its body trembled as if in anticipation of flight.

Dougald said, 'I liked the way you got that into the story that Gnapun and the leader were brothers. Those two brothers, you know, the sons of the leader who were bringing the sheep up through the scrubs? They didn't join in with the retribution afterwards but gave shelter to the messengers' people who survived the killing that went on in the days and months after the massacre. Years later those two boys had fellers working on that place with them that they knew had probably been involved in the massacre of their own family. They accepted something deeper than a need for revenge about what happened that day between their father's party and the local people. I think their dad would have been proud of the way they acted.' He fell silent, looking in over the lip of the partially dismantled wall. 'Gnapun remained a stranger to his people. After the massacre he took a woman to live with him and they had my grandfather. The three of them lived up here on their own until old Gnapun died. After his death my great-grandmother moved down into the valley, and my grandad began working for the stations around the place. I think he went over to that country one time and did some fencing on that place where the massacre was. When Gnapun was old he must have regretted the deaths of those people. Only a young man could do something like he did that day.' He was silent. Then he said, 'He is my hero.'

He seemed to wait for me to say something. 'I had an uncle,' I said, and as I said it I realised that my uncle had not been one of my ghosts last night. 'He too loved his land and lived and died alone for the sake of it. I am the only one who remembers him now. I believe he also came to prefer his solitude to the company of other men, though I don't know what led him to that. He did not have Gnapun's reason for it.'

'Gnapun had to live with what he had done,' Dougald said. 'Old men don't make good killers.'

We stood a while longer, then Dougald said, 'We'd better close her up and get going.'

I paused on the way down and looked back at the wall of stones that Dougald and I had carefully set in place again. They would remain undisturbed there long after he and I were dead. I turned away and followed him and his pale bitch down the incline. Stumbling over loose rocks in my town shoes, and flailing his mother's stick in the air and letting out a yelp whenever my ankle went over, I followed him down the mountain. It took us less than two hours to reach the camp. The two brown dogs were lying in the shade waiting for us at the truck. Dougald lit a fire and made a brew of tea and we looked at each other and smiled to think what we had done.

Schlüterstrasse

20

Remembering Mount Nebo

It was after midnight and I was still at my desk. I was looking out of the window, remembering Mount Nebo. The chestnut trees were in new leaf and the rain was coming down so softly through the streetlights the drops drifted as if snow was falling. The street was deserted. It was the best time, and I was content to be alone. I had restored Winifred's photograph to its former place on my desk and had set Dougald's battered copy of Leichhardt's *Journal* beside her. Dougald's mother's stick was propped in the corner within reach beside my chair. In ten days Vita would be with me again. She was to attend the annual conference, and afterwards we planned to travel and to see something of Europe together. As she had feared, her friendship with her new boyfriend of the narrow shoulders had not blossomed and once again she was waiting for the black prince to rescue her from spinsterhood.

I was remembering a certain day after Dougald and I had returned from our expedition to Gnapun's cave. We were to go to Sydney together and he had asked me to cut his hair. I set a chair out in the yard in readiness for this operation and was sitting at the kitchen table looking out the door waiting for him to finish feeding the hens. The two brown dogs were sprawled on the concrete in the shade of the gum tree. I watched Dougald making his way up the path towards the hen run, the blue plastic bucket of mash in the crook of his arm. He had aged greatly since our return and I was concerned about him. He was wearing his blue overalls and a brown beanie. He had lost weight and the overalls hung on him loosely, as if he had borrowed them from a bigger man. When he reached the hen run he stood at the wire gate, steadying himself against the post, gathering his strength. It was clear to me that he had begun to fail and had not recovered from the hardships of the journey into the escarpments. It surprised me that my own health had not suffered any lasting setback from the experience. I watched him lean and fumble with the latch on the wire gate to the hen run. The gatepost sagged and the latch was inclined to catch. The post needed re-setting and the wire tightening. He had spoken of his intention to make these repairs and I had said I would help him. But I am confident neither of us believed we would ever do it. Sitting there watching him, I thought how one day soon the hens would be gone and the old wire enclosure would be overgrown by blackberries, or by one of those thorny bushes that had flourished since the death of the goat. He had the gate open and rested for a breath before stepping into the enclosure. His bitch remained outside, guarding the opening. But there was no need for her to guard it, as the hens were fussing around Dougald's boots. He tipped the mash along the length of the trough for them, taking care not to spill any into the dust. I watched him making his way back along the path. Perhaps, after all, I had caught a glimpse of the Promised Land from Mount Nebo. He was my hero. The end came swiftly.

We were in Sydney staying with Vita. I was to fly home to Germany within the week. He promised to visit me in the summer, when we would be tourists together for a while. We were at a restaurant overlooking the beach in Manly having lunch with Vita and some of her friends, when he leaned and touched my arm and murmured that he was not well. I knew at once there must be something seriously amiss and I had the waiter call a taxi immediately. Dougald collapsed before the taxi arrived. He survived for three days, then suffered a second, more severe collapse. Vita and I were with him in St Vincent's Hospital when he died. Before his second stroke—if that is what it was that felled him in the end, for the doctors did not seem sure of how to name his malady— he said to me, 'It's time for me to go over to the Old People, old mate.' I understood that he was not unhappy with this death and that he even welcomed it. Vita was distraught. It was her first intimate loss. At the funeral she clung to me and wept helplessly on my shoulder throughout the service. That night she said to me, 'I want to know everything. You must tell me every- thing.' I promised her that once I was home in Hamburg I would write an account for her of my journey with Dougald into the escarpments of the Expedition Range. I gave her my journal to read that night and in the morn- ing she said 'Massacre' made up for the shitty paper I had written for the Hamburg conference. 'But I still want to know everything. Uncle Dougald never told me any of that stuff about Gnapun.'

I began writing this account for Vita six months ago.
I was working on it for only a few days when I realised
the story of our journey to Gnapun's cave told in isolation
would not offer her the true dimensions of the experience
for either Dougald or for myself. So I began with the day
Vita and I met, the day I had planned to be my last, until
she convinced me I had another life to live. Now I was
impatient to see her again and was wondering what new
challenge she would set for me.

The rain had stopped. I reached for my stick and got
up and switched off the study light and stumped out into
the sitting room. I poured myself a shot of whisky—yes,
I have become a whisky drinker in my old age, but I take
it without the tablets. Perhaps I would disclose my next
task to Vita before she had a chance to suggest it to me.
I was no longer the grieving, defeated old man she had
rescued from suicide that day, but had perhaps become
more the man she had thought worth rescuing. To write
of my father's war, to venture into the darkness of my
family's silence, no longer seemed to me to be utterly
taboo and an impossibility. Whether my father's story
might best be written as history or as fiction, however,
I could not yet say. There was much work to be done and I
was looking forward to getting started on it.

I switched on the television. There was an old Greek film on. It had evidently been running for some time. After I had been watching it for a few minutes I remembered that Winifred and I had seen the film together more than thirty years earlier. Although I had forgotten much of the story, I enjoyed the broken fragment of the film as greatly as I had once enjoyed the whole of it. But there, it is all fragments, and in the midst of it we may know this sense of completion.

Acknowledgments

I wish to thank the Australia Council for the generous grant of a two-year fellowship during the writing of this book.

I would like to express my heartfelt gratitude to my friends Frank Budby, elder of the Barada people, and Col McLennan, elder of the Jangga, and to Liz Hatté, for their encouragement and enthusiasm during the writing not only of this book but also of my earlier novel, *Journey to the Stone Country*. Without their confidence and friendship over the years neither of these books would have been possible. I owe a particular debt to my dear friend Dr Anita Heiss, one of Australia's foremost Indigenous scholars and writers. I take this opportunity to record my gratitude also to Professor Gerd Dose, of Hamburg University, who generously read the manuscript and offered me invaluable advice and encouragement.

Lastly, I wish to thank my wonderful editor, Ali Lavau, and publisher, Annette Barlow, and her splendid team at Allen & Unwin.

The chapter titled 'Massacre' is my own fiction. It is, however, a story that I have based on a real event in Australian history known as the Cullin-la-Ringo massacre. Cullin-la-Ringo is said to have been the largest-ever massacre of white settlers by Indigenous Australians in our history. I first heard the story when I was sixteen and was newly arrived from London in the Central Highlands of Queensland—embarked, so I understood, on the most astonishing adventure of my life. I was working as a stockman on a cattle station near Springsure, not far from Cullin-la-Ringo, the station on which the massacre took place on 17 October 1861. The massacre was an event that owned then, and to this day I believe still owns, a sacred place in the collective memory of the local station people and their families.

On that fine October day in 1861, every member of the strongest and most well-armed party of white settlers ever to enter the Central Highlands up to that time was killed by the local Aborigines in whose country they had thought to settle. There were nineteen deaths in all. The accounts tell us there were no Aboriginal casualties that day. When I first heard this story as a youth, it seemed to me that the attack on this large party of armed white settlers must have been extraordinarily well planned, and that there must have been an Aboriginal leader of great character and ruthless strategic intelligence behind the planning of it. No mention of such an Aboriginal leader was ever made, however, in the accounts that were told to me, and my earnest inquiries about the existence of such a person at the time were met with a response which implied that, as a newcomer to Australia and in particular to the Central Highlands of Queensland, my question was naive. My private belief, that there must have been such a leader among the Aborigines of those days, persisted. In writing this fiction I have not relied solely on my own memory of the stories I was told in my youth, nor on the results of my contemporary discussions with Aboriginal friends, but have consulted a number of books and articles, some of which have been of great use to me in recovering a sense of the European historical context of the massacre. The most thorough and detailed account is to be found in Les Perrin's assiduously researched *Cullin-la-Ringo: The Triumph and Tragedy of Tommy Wills*, Les Perrin, 1998. Gordon Reid's essay 'From Hornet Bank to Cullin-la-Ringo', in the *Journal of the Royal Historical Society of Queensland*, Vol. XI, No. 2, 1980–81, was of great use to me, as was Henry Reynolds' 'Settlers and Aborigines on the Pastoral Frontier', in *Lectures on North Queensland History*, James Cook University, Townsville 1974, and, lastly, David Carment's 'The Wills Massacre of 1861: Aboriginal–European Conflict on the Colonial Australian Frontier', in the *Journal of Australian Studies*, 6 June 1980.